WITHDRAWN

ALSO BY THOMAS PYNCHON

V.

The Crying of Lot 49

Gravity's Rainbow

SLOW LEARNER

THOMAS PYNCHON

SLOW LEARNER

EARLY STORIES

LITTLE, BROWN AND COMPANY · BOSTON · TORONTO

FIRST EDITION

Quotation from the lyric "A Room with a View" by kind permission
of the Estate of Noel Coward, c/o Michael Imison Playwrights, Ltd.,
New York.

Quotation from *Tropic of Cancer* by Henry Miller by permission
of Grove Press. Copyright © 1961 by Grove Press.

LIBRARY OF CONGRESS CATALOGING IN PUBLICATION DATA

Pynchon, Thomas.
 Slow Learner.

 I. Title.
PS3566.Y55S5   1984   813'.54   84-934
ISBN 0-316-72442-4

MV

Designed by Dede Cummings

Published simultaneously in Canada
by Little, Brown & Company (Canada) Limited

PRINTED IN THE UNITED STATES OF AMERICA

CONTENTS

SLOW LEARNER

INTRODUCTION

A S NEARLY as I can remember, these stories were written between 1958 and 1964. Four of them I wrote when I was in college – the fifth, "The Secret Integration" (1964), is more of a journeyman than an apprentice effort. You may already know what a blow to the ego it can be to have to read over anything you wrote 20 years ago, even cancelled checks. My first reaction, rereading these stories, was *oh my God,* accompanied by physical symptoms we shouldn't dwell upon. My second thought was about some kind of a wall-to-wall rewrite. These two impulses have given way to one of those episodes of middle-aged tranquility, in which I now pretend to have reached a level of clarity about the young writer I was back then. I mean I can't very well just 86 this guy from my life. On the other hand, if through some as yet undeveloped technology I were to run into him today, how comfortable would I feel about lending him money, or for that matter even stepping down the street to have a beer and talk over old times?

[3]

It is only fair to warn even the most kindly disposed of readers that there are some mighty tiresome passages here, juvenile and delinquent too. At the same time, my best hope is that, pretentious, goofy and ill-considered as they get now and then, these stories will still be of use with all their flaws intact, as illustrative of typical problems in entry-level fiction, and cautionary about some practices which younger writers might prefer to avoid.

"The Small Rain" was my first published story. A friend who'd been away in the army the same two years I'd been in the navy supplied the details. The hurricane really happened, and my friend's Signal Corps detachment had the mission described in the story. Most of what I dislike about my writing is present here in embryo, as well as in more advanced forms. I failed to recognize, just for openers, that the main character's problem was real and interesting enough to generate a story on its own. Apparently I felt I had to put on a whole extra overlay of rain images and references to "The Waste Land" and *A Farewell to Arms*. I was operating on the motto "Make it literary," a piece of bad advice I made up all by myself and then took.

Equally embarrassing is the case of Bad Ear to be found marring much of the dialogue, especially toward the end. My sense of regional accents in those days was primitive at best. I had noticed how in the military voices got homogenized into one basic American country voice. Italian street kids from New York started to sound like down-home folks after a while, sailors from Georgia came back off leave complaining that nobody could understand them because they talked like Yankees. Being from the North, what I was hearing as a "southern accent" was really this uniform service accent, and not much else.

I imagined I had heard *oo* for *ow* in civilian voices around Tidewater Virginia, but didn't know that in different areas of this real or civilian South, even in different parts of Virginia, people spoke in a wide number of quite different accents. It is an error also noticeable in movies of the time. My specific problem in the barroom scene is not only that I have a Louisiana girl talking in Tidewater diphthongs imperfectly heard to begin with, but worse, that I insist on making it an element of plot – it makes a difference to Levine, and therefore to what happens in the story. My mistake being to try to show off my ear before I had one.

At the heart of the story, most crucial and worrisome, is the defective way in which my narrator, almost but not quite me, deals with the subject of death. When we speak of "seriousness" in fiction ultimately we are talking about an attitude toward death – how characters may act in its presence, for example, or how they handle it when it isn't so immediate. Everybody knows this, but the subject is hardly ever brought up with younger writers, possibly because given to anyone at the apprentice age, such advice is widely felt to be effort wasted. (I suspect one of the reasons that fantasy and science fiction appeal so much to younger readers is that, when the space and time have been altered to allow characters to travel easily anywhere through the continuum and thus escape physical dangers and timepiece inevitabilities, mortality is so seldom an issue.)

In "The Small Rain" characters are found dealing with death in pre-adult ways. They evade: they sleep late, they seek euphemisms. When they do mention death they try to make with the jokes. Worst of all, they hook it up with sex. You'll notice that toward the end of the story, some kind of sexual encounter appears to take place, though you'd never know it from the text. The language suddenly gets too fancy to read. Maybe this wasn't only my own adolescent nervousness about sex. I think, looking back, that there might have been a general nervousness in the whole college-age subculture. A tendency to self-censorship. It was also the era of *Howl, Lolita, Tropic of Cancer,* and all the excesses of law enforcement that such works provoked. Even the American soft-core pornography available in those days went to absurdly symbolic lengths to avoid describing sex. Today this all seems a dead issue, but back then it was a felt constraint on folks's writing.

What I find interesting about the story now is not so much the quaintness and puerility of attitude as the class angle. Whatever else the peacetime service is good for, it can provide an excellent introduction to the structure of society at large. It becomes evident even to a young mind that often unacknowledged divisions in civilian life find clear and immediate expression in the military distinction between "officers" and "men." One makes the amazing discovery that grown adults walking around with college educations, wearing khaki and brass and charged with heavy-duty responsibilities, can in fact be idiots. And that working-class white hats, while in theory capable of idiocy, are much more apt to display competence, courage, humanity, wisdom, and other virtues associated, by the educated classes, with themselves. Although cast in literary terms, Lardass Levine's conflict in this story is about where to put his loyalties. Being an unpolitical '50's student, I was unaware of this at the time – but in hind-sight I think I was working out of a dilemma that most of us writing then had, in some way, to deal with.

At the simplest level, it had to do with language. We were encouraged from many directions – Kerouac and the Beat writers, the diction of Saul Bellow in *The Adventures of Augie March,* emerging voices like those of Herbert Gold and Philip Roth – to see how at least two very distinct kinds of English could be allowed in fiction to coexist. Allowed! It was actually OK to write like this! Who knew? The effect was exciting, liberating, strongly positive. It was not a case of either/or, but an expansion of possibilities. I don't think we were consciously groping after any synthesis, although perhaps we should have been. The success of the "new left" later in the '60's was to be limited by the failure of college kids and blue-collar workers to get together politically. One reason was the presence of real, invisible class force fields in the way of communication between the two groups.

The conflict in those days was, like most everything else, muted. In its literary version it shaped up as traditional vs. Beat fiction. Although far away, one of the theatres of action we kept hearing about was at the University of Chicago. There was a "Chicago School" of literary criticism, for example, which had a lot of people's attention and respect. At the same time, there had been a shakeup at the *Chicago Review* which resulted in the Beat-oriented *Big Table* magazine. "What happened at Chicago" became shorthand for some unimaginable subversive threat. There were many other such disputes. Against the undeniable power of tradition, we were attracted by such centrifugal lures as Norman Mailer's essay "The White Negro," the wide availability of recorded jazz, and a book I still believe is one of the great American novels, *On the Road,* by Jack Kerouac.

A collateral effect, for me anyway, was that of Helen Waddell's *The Wandering Scholars,* reprinted in the early '50's, an account of the young poets of the Middle Ages who left the monasteries in large numbers and took to the roads of Europe, celebrating in song the wider range of life to be found outside their academic walls. Given the university environment of the time, the parallels weren't hard to see. Not that college life was dull, exactly, but thanks to all these alternative lowlife data that kept filtering insidiously through the ivy, we had begun to get a sense of that other world humming along out there. Some of us couldn't resist the temptation to go out and see what was happening. Enough of us then came back inside with firsthand news to encourage others to try it too – a preview of the mass college dropouts of the '60's.

I enjoyed only a glancing acquaintance with the Beat movement. Like others, I spent a lot of time in jazz clubs, nursing the two-beer minimum. I put on hornrimmed sunglasses at night. I went to parties in lofts where girls wore strange attire. I was hugely tickled by all forms of marijuana humor, though the talk back then was in inverse relation to the availability of that useful substance. In 1956, in Norfolk, Virginia, I had wandered into a bookstore and discovered issue one of the *Evergreen Review,* then an early forum for Beat sensibility. It was an eye-opener. I was in the navy at the time, but I already knew people who would sit in circles on the deck and sing perfectly, in parts, all those early rock 'n' roll songs, who played bongos and saxophones, who had felt honest grief when Bird and later Clifford Brown died. By the time I got back to college, I found academic people deeply alarmed over the *cover* of the *Evergreen Review* then current, not to mention what was inside. It looked as if the attitude of some literary folks toward the Beat generation was the same as that of certain officers on my ship toward Elvis Presley. They used to approach those among ship's company who seemed likely sources – combed their hair like Elvis, for example. "What's his message?" they'd interrogate anxiously. "What does he want?"

We were at a transition point, a strange post-Beat passage of cultural time, with our loyalties divided. As bop and rock 'n' roll were to swing music and postwar pop, so was this new writing to the more established modernist tradition we were being exposed to then in college. Unfortunately there were no more primary choices for us to make. We were onlookers: the parade had gone by and we were already getting everything secondhand, consumers of what the media of the time were supplying us. This didn't prevent us from adopting Beat postures and props, and eventually as post-Beats coming to see deeper into what, after all, was a sane and decent affirmation of what we all want to believe about American values. When the hippie resurgence came along ten years later, there was, for a while anyway, a sense of nostalgia and vindication. Beat prophets were resurrected, people started playing alto sax riffs on electric guitars, the wisdom of the East came back in fashion. It was the same, only different.

On the negative side, however, both forms of the movement placed too much emphasis on youth, including the eternal variety. Youth of course was wasted on me at the time, but I bring up the puerility angle again because, along with imperfectly developed attitudes about sex and death, we may also note how easily some of my adolescent values were able to creep in and wreck an otherwise sympathetic character. Such is the unhappy case with Dennis Flange, in "Low-lands." In a way this is more of a character sketch than a story. Old Dennis doesn't "grow" much in the course of it. He remains static, his fantasies become embarrassingly vivid, that's about all that happens. A brightening of focus maybe, but no problem resolution and so not much movement or life.

It is no secret nowadays, particularly to women, that many American males, even those of middle-aged appearance, wearing suits and holding down jobs, are in fact, incredible as it sounds, still small boys inside. Flange is this type of a character, although when I wrote this story I thought he was pretty cool. He wants children – why isn't made clear – but not at the price of developing any real life shared with an adult woman. His solution to this is Nerissa, a woman with the size and demeanor of a child. I can't remember for sure, but it looks like I wanted some ambiguity here about whether or not she was only a creature of his fantasies. It would be easy to say that Dennis's problem was my problem, and that I was putting it off on him. Whatever's fair – but the problem *could* have been more general. At that time I had no direct experience with either marriage or parenting, and maybe I was picking up on male attitudes that were then in the air – more documentably, inside the pages of men's magazines, *Playboy* in particular. I don't think this magazine was the projection, exclusively, of its publisher's private values: if American men had not widely shared such values, *Playboy* would have quickly failed and faded from the scene.

Oddly enough, I had not intended this to be Dennis's story at all – he was supposed to have been a straight man for Pig Bodine. The counterpart in real life to this unwholesome bluejacket was actually my starting point. I had heard the honeymoon story when I was in the navy, from a gunner's mate on my ship. We were out on shore patrol duty in Portsmouth, Virginia. Our beat was a desolate piece of shipyard perimeter – chain link fences, railroad spurs – and the night was inhospitably cold, with no ill-behaved sailors abroad for us to regulate. So to my shipmate, as senior member of the patrol, fell the obligation to pass the time telling sea stories, and this was one of them. What had actually happened to him on his own honeymoon is what I had happen to Dennis Flange. I was heavily amused not so much at the content of the story as at the more abstract notion that anybody would behave that way. As it turned out, my partner's drinking companion figured in a wide body of shipboard anecdote. Transferred before my time to shore duty someplace, he had become a legend. I finally did get to see him the day before I was discharged, mustering in the early morning outside a barracks at the Norfolk naval base. The minute I caught sight of him, before I heard him answer to his name, I swear I had the strange ESP knowledge that that's who he was. Not to overdramatize the moment – but because I still like Pig Bodine so much, having brought the character in a time or two since in novels, it's pleasant to recall that our paths really did cross in this apparitional way.

Modern readers will be, at least, put off by an unacceptable level of racist, sexist and proto-Fascist talk throughout this story. I wish I could say that this is only Pig Bodine's voice, but, sad to say, it was also my own at the time. The best I can say for it now is that, for its time, it is probably authentic enough. John Kennedy's role model James Bond was about to make his name by kicking third-world people around, another extension of the boy's adventure tales a lot of us grew up reading. There had prevailed for a while a set of assumptions and distinctions, unvoiced and unquestioned, best captured years later in the '70's television character Archie Bunker.

It may yet turn out that racial differences are not as basic as questions of money and power, but have served a useful purpose, often in the interest of those who deplore them most, in keeping us divided and so relatively poor and powerless. This having been said, however, the narrative voice in this story here remains that of a smart-assed jerk who didn't know any better, and I apologize for it.

Disagreeable as I find "Low-lands" now, it's nothing compared to my bleakness of heart when I have to look at "Entropy." The story is a fine example of a procedural error beginning writers are always being cautioned against. It is simply wrong to begin with a theme, symbol or other abstract unifying agent, and then try to force characters and events to conform to it. By contrast, the characters in "Low-lands," though problematic in other ways, were at least where I began from, bringing the theoretical stuff in later, just to give the project a look of educated class. Otherwise it would only have been about a number of unpleasant people failing to resolve difficulties in their lives, and who needs that? Hence, adventitious lectures about tale-telling and geometry.

Because the story has been anthologized a couple-three times, people think I know more about the subject of entropy than I really do. Even the normally unhoodwink-able Donald Barthelme has suggested in a magazine inter-view that I had some kind of proprietary handle on it. Well, according to the *OED* the word was coined in 1865 by Rudolf Clausius, on the model of the word "energy," which he took to be Greek for "work-contents." Entropy, or "transformation-contents" was introduced as a way of examining the changes a heat engine went through in a typical cycle, the transformation being heat into work. If Clausius had stuck to his native German and called it

Verwandlungsinhalt instead, it could have had an entirely different impact. As it was, after having been worked with in a restrained way for the next 70 or 80 years, entropy got picked up on by some communication theorists and given the cosmic moral twist it continues to enjoy in current usage. I happened to read Norbert Wiener's *The Human Use of Human Beings* (a rewrite for the interested layman of his more technical *Cybernetics*) at about the same time as *The Education of Henry Adams,* and the "theme" of the story is mostly derivative of what these two men had to say. A pose I found congenial in those days – fairly common, I hope, among pre-adults – was that of somber glee at any idea of mass destruction or decline. The modern political thriller genre, in fact, has been known to cash in on such visions of death made large-scale or glamorous. Given my undergraduate mood, Adams's sense of power out of control, coupled with Wiener's spectacle of universal heat-death and mathematical stillness, seemed just the ticket. But the distance and grandiosity of this led me to short-change the humans in the story. I think they come off as synthetic, insufficiently alive. The marital crisis described is once again, like the Flanges', unconvincingly simplified. The lesson is sad, as Dion always sez, but true: get too conceptual, too cute and remote, and your characters die on the page.

For a while all I worried about was that I'd set things up in terms of temperature and not energy. As I read more about the subject later, I came to see that this had not been such a bad tactic. But do not underestimate the shallowness of my understanding. For instance, I chose 37 degrees Fahrenheit for an equilibrium point because 37 degrees Celsius is the temperature of the human body. Cute, huh?

Further, it turns out that not everyone has taken such a dim view of entropy. Again according to the *OED*, Clerk Maxwell and P. G. Tait used it, for a while at least, in a sense opposite to that of Clausius: as a measure of energy available, not unavailable, for work. Willard Gibbs, who in this country a century ago developed the property at theoretical length, thought of it, in diagram form anyway, as an aid to popularizing the science of thermodynamics, in particular its second law.

What strikes me nowadays about the story is not so much its thermodynamical gloom as the way it reflects how the '50's were for some folks. I suppose it is as close to a Beat story as anything I was writing then, although I thought I was sophisticating the Beat spirit with second-hand science. I wrote "Entropy" in '58 or '59 – when I talk about '57 in the story as "back then" I am being almost sarcastic. One year of those times was much like another. One of the most pernicious effects of the '50's was to convince the people growing up during them that it would last forever. Until John Kennedy, then perceived as a congressional upstart with a strange haircut, began to get some attention, there was a lot of aimlessness going around. While Eisenhower was in, there seemed no reason why it should all not just go on as it was.

Since I wrote this story I have kept trying to understand entropy, but my grasp becomes less sure the more I read. I've been able to follow the *OED* definitions, and the way Isaac Asimov explains it, and even some of the math. But the qualities and quantities will not come together to form a unified notion in my head. It is cold comfort to find out that Gibbs himself anticipated the problem, when he described entropy in its written form as "far-fetched . . . obscure and difficult of comprehension." When I think about the property nowadays, it is more and more in connection with time, that human one-way time we're all stuck with locally here, and which terminates, it is said, in death. Certain processes, not only thermodynamic ones but also those of a medical nature, can often not be reversed. Sooner or later we all find this out, from the inside.

Such considerations were largely absent when I wrote "Entropy." I was more concerned with committing on paper a variety of abuses, such as overwriting. I will spare everybody a detailed discussion of all the overwriting that occurs in these stories, except to mention how distressed I am at the number of tendrils that keep showing up. I still don't even know for sure what a tendril is. I think I took the word from T. S. Eliot. I have nothing against tendrils personally, but my overuse of the word is a good example of what can happen when you spend too much time and energy on words alone. This advice has been given often and more compellingly elsewhere, but my specific piece of wrong procedure back then was, incredibly, to browse through the thesaurus and note words that sounded cool, hip, or likely to produce an effect, usually that of making me look good, without then taking the trouble to go and find out in the dictionary what they meant. If this sounds stupid, it is. I mention it only on the chance that others may be doing it even as we speak, and be able to profit from my error.

This same free advice can also be applied to items of information. Everybody gets told to write about what they know. The trouble with many of us is that at the earlier stages of life we think we know everything – or to put it more usefully, we are often unaware of the scope and structure of our ignorance. Ignorance is not just a blank space on a person's mental map. It has contours and coherence, and for all I know rules of operation as well. So as a corollary to writing about what we know, maybe we should add getting familiar with our ignorance, and the possibilities therein for ruining a good story. Opera librettos, movies and television drama are allowed to get away with all kinds of errors in detail. Too much time in front of the Tube and a writer can get to believing the same thing about fiction. Not so. Though it may not be wrong absolutely to make up, as I still do, what I don't know or am too lazy to find out, phony data are more often than not deployed in places sensitive enough to make a difference, thereby losing what marginal charm they may have possessed outside of the story's context. Witness an example from "Entropy." In the character of Callisto I was trying for a sort of world-weary Middle-European effect, and put in the phrase *grippe espagnole,* which I had seen on some liner notes to a recording of Stravinsky's *L'Histoire du Soldat.* I must have thought this was some kind of post–World War I spiritual malaise or something. Come to find out it means what it says, Spanish influenza, and the reference I lifted was really to the worldwide flu epidemic that followed the war.

The lesson here, obvious but now and then overlooked, is just to corroborate one's data, in particular those acquired casually, such as through hearsay or off the backs of record albums. We have, after all, recently moved into an era when, at least in principle, everybody can share an inconceivably enormous amount of information, just by stroking a few keys on a terminal. There are no longer any excuses for small stupid mistakes, and I hope this also leads to much more inhibition about stealing data on the chance that no one will catch it.

Fascinating topic, literary theft. As in the penal code, there are degrees. These range from plagiarism down to only being derivative, but all are forms of wrong procedure. If, on the other hand, you believe that nothing is original and that all writers "borrow" from "sources," there still remains the question of credit lines or acknowledgements. It wasn't till "Under the Rose" (1959) that I could bring myself, even indirectly, to credit guidebook eponym Karl Baedeker, whose guide to Egypt for 1899 was the major "source" for the story.

I spotted this book in the Cornell Co-op. All fall and winter I had been having writer's block. I was taking a writing seminar run by Baxter Hathaway. Having returned that semester after some time off, he was an unknown quantity, and terrified me. The course had been going on for some time, and I hadn't handed in a thing. "Come on," people advised me, "he's a nice guy. Don't worry about it." Were they kidding, or what? It was getting to be a major problem. Finally about halfway through the semester there arrived in the mail one of those cartoon cards, showing a toilet stall covered with graffiti. "You've practiced long enough," it said – open the card – "Now write!" It was signed "Baxter Hathaway." Could I, even as I laid down cash for it at the cash register, have been subconsciously planning to loot this faded red volume for the contents of a story?

Could Willy Sutton rob a safe? Loot the Baedeker I did, all the details of a time and place I had never been to, right down to the names of the diplomatic corps. Who'd make up a name like Khevenhüller-Metsch? Lest others become as enchanted as I was and have continued to be with this technique, let me point out that it is a lousy way to go about writing a story. The problem here is like the problem with "Entropy": beginning with something abstract – a thermodynamic coinage or the data in a guidebook – and only then going on to try to develop plot and characters. This is simply, as we say in the profession, ass backwards. Without some grounding in human reality, you are apt to be left only with another apprentice exercise, which is what this uncomfortably resembles.

I was also able to steal, or let us say "derive," in more subtle ways. I had grown up reading a lot of spy fiction, novels of intrigue, notably those of John Buchan. The only book of his that anyone remembers now is *The Thirty-nine Steps,* but he wrote half a dozen more just as good or better. They were all in my hometown library. So were E. Phillips Oppenheim, Helen MacInnes, Geoffrey Household, and many others as well. The net effect was eventually to build up in my uncritical brain a peculiar shadowy vision of the history preceding the two world wars. Political decision-making and official documents did not figure in this nearly as much as lurking, spying, false identities, psychological games. Much later I got around to two other mighty influences, Edmund Wilson's *To the Finland Station* and Machiavelli's *The Prince,* which helped me to develop the interesting question underlying the story – is history personal or statistical? My reading at the time also included many Victorians, allowing World War I in my imagination to assume the shape of that attractive nuisance so dear to adolescent minds, the apocalyptic showdown.

I don't mean to make light of this. Our common nightmare The Bomb is in there too. It was bad enough in '59 and is much worse now, as the level of danger has continued to grow. There was never anything subliminal about it, then or now. Except for that succession of the criminally insane who have enjoyed power since 1945, including the power to do something about it, most of the rest of us poor sheep have always been stuck with simple, standard fear. I think we all have tried to deal with this slow escalation of our helplessness and terror in the few ways open to us, from not thinking about it to going crazy from it. Somewhere on this spectrum of impotence is writing fiction about it – occasionally, as here, offset to a more colorful time and place.

So, if only for its feeble good intentions, I am less annoyed with "Under the Rose" than with the earlier stuff. I think the characters are a little better, no longer just lying there on the slab but beginning at least to twitch some and blink their eyes open, although their dialogue still suffers from my perennial Bad Ear. Thanks to the relentless efforts of the Public Broadcast System, everyone these days is hyperfamiliar with the furthest nuances of English as spoken by the English. In my day I had to depend on movies and radio, which as sources then were not 100% reliable. Hence all the pip-pip and jolly-ho business, which to a modern reader comes across as stereotyped and inauthentic. Readers may also feel shorted because of how, more than anyone, the masterful John le Carré has upped the ante for the whole genre. Today we expect a complexity of plot and depth of character which are missing from my effort here. Most of it, happily, is chase scenes, for which I remain a dedicated sucker – it is one piece of puerility I am unable to let go of. May Road Runner cartoons never vanish from the video waves, is my attitude.

Attentive fans of Shakespeare will notice that the name Porpentine is lifted from *Hamlet,* I, v. It is an early form of "porcupine." The name Moldweorp is Old Teutonic for "mole" – the animal, not the infiltrator. I thought it would be a cute idea for people named after two amiable fuzzy critters to be duking it out over the fate of Europe.

Less conscientiously, there is also an echo of the name of the reluctant spy character Wormold, in Graham Greene's *Our Man in Havana,* then recently published.

Another influence in "Under the Rose," too recent for me then to abuse to the extent I have done since, is Surrealism. I had been taking one of those elective courses in Modern Art, and it was the Surrealists who'd really caught my attention. Having as yet virtually no access to my dream life, I missed the main point of the movement, and became fascinated instead with the simple idea that one could combine inside the same frame elements not normally found together to produce illogical and startling effects. What I had to learn later on was the necessity of managing this procedure with some degree of care and skill: any old combination of details will not do. Spike Jones, Jr., whose father's orchestral recordings had a deep and indelible effect on me as a child, said once in an interview, "One of the things that people don't realize about Dad's kind of music is, when you replace a C-sharp with a gunshot, it has to be a C-sharp gunshot or it sounds awful."

I was to get even worse at this, as is evident from the junkshop or randomly assembled quality to many of the scenes in "The Secret Integration." But because I like more than dislike this story, I sometimes will blame it more on the cluttered way that items accumulate in the rooms of memory. Like "Low-lands." this is a hometown story, one of the few times I tried to write directly out of the landscape and the experiences I grew up with. I mistakenly thought of Long Island then as a giant and featureless sandbar, without history, someplace to get away from but not to feel very connected to. It is interesting that in both stories I imposed on what I felt to be blank space a set of more complicated topographies.

Perhaps I felt this was a way to make the place a little more exotic.

Not only did I complicate this Long Island space, but I also drew a line around the whole neighborhood, picked it up and shifted it all to the Berkshires, where I still have never been. The old Baedeker trick again. This time I found the details I needed in the regional guide to the Berkshires put out in the 1930's by the Federal Writers Project of the WPA. This is one of an excellent set of state and regional volumes, which may still be available in libraries. They make instructive and pleasurable reading. In fact, there is some stuff in the Berkshire book so good, so rich in detail and deep in feeling, that even I was ashamed to steal from it.

Why I adopted such a strategy of transfer is no longer clear to me. Displacing my personal experience off into other environments went back at least as far as "The Small Rain." Part of this was an unkind impatience with fiction I felt then to be "too autobiographical." Somewhere I had come up with the notion that one's personal life had nothing to do with fiction, when the truth, as everyone knows, is nearly the direct opposite. Moreover, contrary evidence was all around me, though I chose to ignore it, for in fact the fiction both published and unpublished that moved and pleased me then as now was precisely that which had been made luminous, undeniably authentic by having been found and taken up, always at a cost, from deeper, more shared levels of the life we all really live. I hate to think that I didn't, however defectively, understand this. Maybe the rent was just too high. In any case, stupid kid, I preferred fancy footwork instead.

Then again, maybe another factor in it was just claustrophobia. I wasn't the only one writing then who felt some need to stretch, to step out. It may have gone back to the sense of academic enclosure we felt which had lent such appeal to the American picaresque life the Beat writers seemed to us to be leading. Apprentices in all fields and times are restless to be journeymen.

By the time I wrote "The Secret Integration" I was embarked on this phase of the business. I had published a novel and thought I knew a thing or two, but for the first time I believe I was also beginning to shut up and listen to the American voices around me, even to shift my eyes away from printed sources and take a look at American nonverbal reality. I was out on the road at last, getting to visit the places Kerouac had written about. These towns and Greyhound voices and fleabag hotels have found their way into this story, and I am pretty content with how it holds up.

Not that it's perfect, understand, not by a long shot. The kids, for example, seem in some areas to be not very bright, certainly not a patch on the kids of the '80's. I could also with an easy mind see axed much of the story's less responsible Surrealism. Still, there are parts of it I can't believe I wrote. Sometime in the last couple of decades, some company of elves must have snuck in and had a crack at it. As is clear from the up-and-down shape of my learning curve, however, it was too much to expect that I'd keep on for long in this positive or professional direction. The next story I wrote was "The Crying of Lot 49," which was marketed as a "novel," and in which I seem to have forgotten most of what I thought I'd learned up till then.

Most likely, much of my feeling for this last story can be traced to ordinary nostalgia for this time in my life, for the writer who seemed then to be emerging, with his bad habits, dumb theories and occasional moments of productive silence in which he may have begun to get a glimpse of how it was done. What is most appealing about young folks, after all, is the changes, not the still photograph of finished character but the movie, the soul in flux. Maybe this small attachment to my past is only another case of what Frank Zappa calls a bunch of old guys sitting around playing rock 'n' roll. But as we all know, rock 'n' roll will never die, and education too, as Henry Adams always sez, keeps going on forever.

THE SMALL RAIN

OUTSIDE, the company area broiled slowly under the sun. The air was soggy, hanging motionless. The sun glared yellow off the sand around the barracks that housed the company's radio section. There was no one inside except an orderly leaning drowsy against the wall, smoking, and an inert figure in fatigues lying on a bunk, reading a paperback. The orderly yawned and spat outside into the hot sand and the figure in the bunk, whose name was Levine, turned a page and rearranged the pillow under his head. Somewhere a big mosquito was buzzing against a windowpane and somewhere else there was a radio tuned to a rock 'n' roll station in Leesville, and outside jeeps and deuce-and-a-halfs were scurrying or rumbling back and forth constantly. This was Fort Roach, Louisiana, back around mid-July of '57. Nathan "Lardass" Levine, specialist 3/C, has been assigned to the same battalion, the same company, the same bunk, for 13 months now, going on 14. Roach being the kind of installation it was, this circumstance might have driven more ordinary men to the point of suicide or at least

insanity; indeed, according to certain more or less sup-
pressed army statistics, it often did. Levine, however,
was not quite ordinary. He was one of the few men
outside of those bucking for section eight who actually
liked Ft. Roach. He had quietly and unobtrusively gone
native: the angular edges of his Bronx accent had been
dulled and softened into a modified drawl; he had found
that white lightning, usually straight or else mixed with
whatever happened to be coming out of the company
Coke machine at the time, was in its way as agreeable as
scotch on the rocks; he now listened to hillbilly groups
in bars in the neighboring towns as raptly as he had once
dug Lester Young or Gerry Mulligan at Birdland. He
was well over six feet and loose-jointed, but what certain
coeds at City had once described as a plowboy physique,
rawboned and taut-muscled, had run to flab after three
years of avoiding work details. He had a fine beer belly
now, in which he maintained a certain pride, and a large
behind which he was not so proud of, which had earned
him his nickname.

The orderly flipped the butt of his cigarette out into
the sand and said, "Look who's coming."

"If it's the general tell him I'm sleeping," Levine said.
He lit a cigarette and yawned.

"No," the orderly said, "it's Twinkletoes." He leaned
back on the wall again and closed his eyes. There was a
patter of little feet on the porch and a Virginia accent
said, "Capucci, you worthless bastard." The orderly
opened his eyes. "Get laid," he said. Twinkletoes Dugan
the company clerk came in and approached Levine with
an ill-natured pout on his lips. "Who's got that whore
book after you, Levine," he said. Levine, who was using
his helmet liner for an ashtray, flicked his cigarette. "The
GI can I reckon," he smiled. The pout became a thin line.
"Lieutenant wants to see you," Dugan said, "so get off

your lard ass and over to the orderly room." Levine turned another page and started reading. "Hey," the company clerk said. Levine smiled vaguely. Dugan was a draftee. He had busted out of the University of Virginia after two years and like many company clerks had a sadistic streak in him. There were a lot of other nice things about Dugan. He held as self-evident truths, for example, that the NAACP was a Communist cabal dedicated to 100% intermarriage of the White and Negro races, and that the Virginia gentleman was in reality the *Übermensch*, come at last, prevented from fulfilling his high destiny only by the malevolent plotting of the New York Jews. Mainly on account of the latter he and Levine did not get along too well.

"Lieutenant wants to see me," Levine said. "Don't tell me you got my leave papers already. Hell –" he looked at his watch – "it's only a little after 11. Congratulations, Dugan. 5½ hours ahead of time." He shook his head admiringly. Dugan smirked. "I don't think it's about your leave. In fact you might have to wait awhile on that."

Levine put the book down and stubbed out his cigarette in the helmet liner. He looked up at the ceiling. "Jesus Christ," he said quietly, "what did I do now. Don't tell me they're going to put me in jail. Not again."

"It's only been a couple weeks since your last summary, hasn't it," the clerk said. Levine knew this gambit. He figured Dugan had given up a long time ago trying to make him sweat. But guys like that, he supposed, never gave up. "So get out of your bunk, is all I'm saying," Dugan said. He pronounced "out" like "oot." This irritated Levine. He picked up the book and began to read. "All right," he said, flipping a salute. "Go back, white man." Dugan glared at him and finally went away. Apparently he tripped over the orderly's M1 on his way out, because there was a crash and Capucci said, "God, you're an uncoordinated bastard." Levine closed the book, folded it in half, rolled over and stuck it in his back pocket. He lay there for a minute or so watching a cockroach following some private maze across the floor. Finally he yawned and dragged himself off the bunk, dumped the butts and ashes out of the helmet liner onto the floor and put the helmet liner on his head, canted down over his eyes. He squeezed the orderly's head as he went out. "What's shaking?" Capucci said. Levine squinted into the bright heavy air outside. "Oh, the Pentagon, again," he said. "Just won't let me alone."

He shuffled through the sand, feeling the sun already through the helmet liner, toward the building where the orderly room was located. Around the building was a fringe of green, the only grass in the company area. Ahead and to his left he could see the line for early chow already forming by the mess hall. He turned onto the gravel path leading to the orderly room. He expected Dugan to be outside or at least at a window looking for him but when he entered the orderly room the clerk was at his desk in back, typing busily. Levine leaned on the railing in front of the first sergeant's desk. "Hi, Sarge," he said. The first sergeant looked up. "Where the hell were you," he said, "reading a whore book?" "That's right, Sarge," Levine said, "I was studying for sergeant." The first sergeant scowled. "Lieutenant wants to see you," he said.

"So I heard," Levine said. "Where is he?"

"In the day room," the first sergeant said, "with the rest of the men."

"What's going on, Sarge, anything special?"

"Go on in and find out," the sergeant said peevishly. "Jesus Christ, Levine, you ought to know by now, nobody ever tells me anything."

Levine left the orderly room and walked around the building to the day room. Through the screen door he could hear the lieutenant talking. He pushed open the door. The lieutenant and about a dozen PFC's and specialists from Bravo Company were sitting or standing around a table and looking at a map which was stained with coffee cup rings. "DiGrandi and Siegel," the lieutenant was saying, "Rizzo and Baxter —" he looked up and saw Levine. "Levine, you'll be with Picnic." He folded the map carelessly and put it in his back pocket. "Everything straight?" They all nodded. "Okay, that's all till one then. Have the trucks out of the motor pool by then and take off. I'll see you at Lake Charles." He put on his hat and left, letting the screen door bang behind him. "Coke time," Rizzo said. "Somebody got a weed?" Levine sat down on a table and said, "What's happening."

"Oh Christ," Baxter said. He was a little blond-haired farm kid from Pennsylvania. "Welcome to the club, Levine. It's the goddam Cajuns again. They put up all kinds of signs, sure. Dogs and Army Stay off the Grass and all. But the minute the least little thing screws up, who do they go crying to."

"131st Signal Battalion," Rizzo said, "is who."

"Where-all we going at one," Levine said. Picnic got up from where he was sitting and headed for the Coke machine. "Someplace out by Lake Charles," he said. "They had a storm or something. Lines are down." He put a nickel in and as usual nothing happened. "Bravo company to the rescue." His voice became soothing, caressing. "Come on, *bebi*," he said to the Coke machine and kicked it viciously. Nothing happened. "Be careful you don't tilt it," Baxter said. Picnic hammered on the machine in certain carefully selected spots. Something clicked and two streams, one of carbonated water and

one of Coke syrup, began to flow out. Just before they
shut off, an empty cup dropped down and got covered
on the outside with syrup. "Oh god, you're cute," Picnic
said. "It's neurotic," Rizzo said. "The heat has driven it
crazy." They talked for a while, speculating and cursing
the Cajuns and the army, smoking and drinking Cokes,
till finally Levine stood up and put his hands in his pockets
letting his gut bulge out. "Well," he said, "I reckon I'll
go pack."

"Wait a minute," Picnic said. "I'll go with you." They
went out the screen door and back down the gravel path
to the sand area in front of Radio section's barracks.
They trudged across the sand, sweating in the windless
air and the hot yellow sun. "Never a dull moment, Benny,"
Levine said. "Oh Jesus," Picnic said. They went in the
barracks doing the stockade shuffle and when Capucci
asked what was happening they gave him the finger,
simultaneously and precisely, like a vaudeville team.

Levine got his laundry bag out and started throwing
fatigues, skivvies and socks into it. He put his shaving kit
in last and then as an afterthought wedged an old blue
baseball cap down the side. He stood there frowning for
a while and then said. "Hey Picnic."

"Yo," Picnic said from the other end of the barracks.

"*I* can't go on this detail. I got leave starting at 4:30."

"So what are you packing for," Picnic said.

"I think maybe what I'll do is go over and see Pierce
about it."

"He's eating, most likely."

"Well we got to go eat anyway. Come on."

They plodded out again into the sun, through the sand,
around to the back door of the mess hall. Lieutenant
Pierce was sitting at an empty table near the serving line.
Levine went over.

"I been thinking," he said.

[*32*]

The lieutenant looked up. "Having trouble about the trucks?" he said. Levine scratched his stomach and tilted the helmet liner back on his head. "Not exactly," he said, "but my leave starts at 4:30 and I was figuring." Pierce dropped the fork he was holding. It hit the tray with a loud clank. "No," he said, "you'll have to wait awhile on that leave, Levine." Levine smiled a big loose idiot's smile that he knew got on the lieutenant's nerves. "Hell," he said, "since when am I so indispensable to the company?" Pierce sighed in annoyance. "Look, you know the situation in this company as well as anybody. And the order says specialists, ace specialists. Unfortunately we don't have any. But you have to do, slobs like you are all we have." Pierce was ROTC, a graduate of MIT. He had just made first lieutenant and was trying hard not to feel his power. When he spoke it was with a precise, dry Beacon Hill accent. "Lieutenant," Levine said, "you were young once. I got this broad in N'Orleans, she's waiting for me. Give youth its day. There's hundreds of specialists better than me." The lieutenant smiled grimly. There was an implicit and mutual recognition of worth between them whenever things like this cropped up. Outwardly neither had any use for the other; but each had the vague sense that they were more alike than either would care to admit, brothers, possibly, under the skin. When Pierce had first arrived at Roach and found out the story on Levine he had tried to talk to him. "You're wasting yourself, Levine," he would say. "Here you are, college graduate, highest IQ in the damn battalion, and what are you doing. Sitting here in the most wretched pesthole in the armed forces, on an ass that gets broader every month. Why don't you go for OCS? You could probably even get into the Point if you wanted. Why did you enlist in the army in the first place?" And Levine would say with a hesitant grin that was neither quite apologetic nor quite scornful, "Well I sort of figured

I'd like to stay an enlisted man and make a career out of it." At first the lieutenant would blow up whenever he said this, get incoherent. Later he would turn and walk away and finally he gave up altogether and gave up talking to Levine. Now he said, "You're in the army, Levine. Leave isn't a right, it's a privilege." Levine stuck his hands in his back pockets. "Ah," he said. "Well, okay."

He turned and walked away slowly, hands in his pockets, over to the tray rack. He got a tray and silverware and went through the line. It was stew again. Thursday always seemed to be stew day. He went over to where Picnic was eating and said, "Guess what."

"I figured," Picnic said. They ate and walked out of the mess hall and about a mile through sand and over concrete, dragging their feet and not talking, just letting the sun glare and work through the helmet liners and hair to the scalp. They got to the motor pool at a quarter to one and found most of the others already there with six ¾-ton trucks with radio equipment in the back. Levine and Picnic got into a truck, Picnic driving, and followed the other trucks up to the company. At the barracks they got their bags and threw them in back.

They headed on a southwesterly direction, through swamp and past farmland. As they got nearer to the town of De Ridder they could see clouds to the south. "Rain?" Picnic said. "Jesus Christ." Levine had put on a pair of sunglasses and was reading the paperback again, something called *Swamp Wench*. "The more I think about it," he said lazily, "the more I think someday I'm gonna give that there lieutenant a punch in the mouth."

"It's a bitch, ain't it," Picnic agreed.

"I mean," Levine said, putting the book face down on his stomach, "Sometimes I almost wish I was back at City. And that's bad."

"Why bad?" Picnic said. "I'd rather be back at the Academy any day than doing this crap."

"No," Levine said frowning, "you don't go back. I only went back once that I can remember and that was to a broad. And that was bad too."

"Yeah," Pic said. "You told me. You should have gone back. I wish I could. Back to the barracks, even, and go to sleep."

"You can sleep anywhere," Levine said. "I can."

At De Ridder they turned south. The clouds massed up, gray and threatening, ahead of them. Around them swamp would stretch out, gray and mossy and foul-smelling, and then give way to poor-looking farmland. "You want to read this after me?" Levine said. "It's pretty good. All about swamps. And this broad that lives in them."

"Really?" Picnic said, looking grimly at the truck ahead of them. "I wish I could find a broad in one of these. I'd build me this shack way out in the middle of one of them, where Uncle would never find me."

"Sure you would," Levine said.

"I know damn well *you* would."

"Till I got tired of it, anyway," Levine said.

"Why don't you settle down, Nathan," Picnic said. "Find a nice quiet girl and go live up north."

"It's the army I'm in love with," Levine said.

"You 30-year men are all alike. Does Pierce still believe all that crap about re-upping?"

"I don't know. I don't believe it, why should he. But then I might be telling the truth. I reckon I'll just wait and see, when the time comes."

They drove on like this for about two hours, dropping off trucks along the way to set up relays back to Roach until on the outskirts of Lake Charles there were only two trucks left. Rizzo, with Baxter, in the truck ahead, waved Levine and Picnic down. The sky was completely overcast now and a small wind was blowing, chilly against their damp fatigues. "Let's find a bar," Rizzo said. "Wait for the lieutenant to catch up." Rizzo was a staff sergeant. He was also the company intellectual. He would lie in his bunk and read things like *Being and Nothingness* and *Form and Value in Modern Poetry,* scorning the westerns, sex novels and whodunnits that his companions kept trying to lend him. He, Picnic and Levine often held long bull sessions at night in the PX or the coffee shop, usually with Rizzo doing most of the talking. They drove into town and found a quiet bar near a high school. There were a couple of schoolkids sitting at the bar but otherwise the place was empty. They got a table near the back and Rizzo headed for the latrine. Baxter headed for the door. "Be back in a minute," he said, "I want to get a paper." Levine sat drinking beer and brooding. He often had this habit of pursing his lips like Marlon Brando and scratching his armpit. Sometimes, depending on his mood, he would make quiet ape noises. "Picnic, wake up," he said finally. "The general's coming."

"General's ass," Picnic said.

"You're just bitter," Rizzo said, coming back. "Be like me, or Lardass there. Happy-go-lucky."

Baxter came running in just then with a newspaper, all excited. "Hey," he said, "we made the headlines." He had a Lake Charles paper, and when he opened it up on the table there was this big banner headline, 250 MISSING IN HURRICANE. "Hurricane?" Picnic said. "Who the hell said anything about a hurricane?"

"Maybe the navy can't get a plane up," Rizzo said, "they want us to find the eye or something."

"I wonder what's going on out there, though," Baxter said, thoughtfully. "Christ, things must be bad if they got no communications at all."

The hurricane, it turned out, had completely annihilated

a small village called Creole, located on an island, or
rather a high area, in the bayou country along the gulf,
about 20 miles from Lake Charles. The whole business
had clearly been a foulup on the part of the Weather
Bureau: Wednesday afternoon, when the inhabitants of
the town had started to evacuate, the bureau had issued
a statement that the hurricane would not arive till Thursday night. It urged them not to crowd the roads. There
was plenty of time. Sometime between midnight and
three Thursday morning the hurricane hit, zeroed in
on Creole. The National Guard was coming, the article
continued, so were the Red Cross, the army and the navy.
They were trying to get planes up from the air force base
in Biloxi but flying conditions were very bad. One of the
big oil companies was contributing a couple of tugboats
to aid in rescue operations. Creole would probably be
declared a disaster area. And so on. They had a few more
beers and talked about the hurricane and everyone agreed
that for the next few days they were probably going to
be working their ass off, and this led to several statements,
obscene and disaffected, about the nature of the U.S.
Army. "Re-up," Rizzo said, "you still got time, you can still
be eligible. *I* got 382 goddam days. Christ, I'll never make
it." Levine smiled. "Shucks," he said, "you're just bitter, is
all." When they got outside it was raining and cooler.
They got in the trucks and splashed back out of town to
the rendezvous point Lieutenant Pierce had arranged.
There was no sign of him yet. Levine and Picnic sat parked,
listening to rain bounce off the roof. Levine pulled *Swamp
Wench* out of his pocket and began reading again.

After a while Rizzo came over and banged on the
window. "The general's coming," he said, pointing down
the road. Through the rain they could make out a jeep
with a muddy figure in khakis driving. The jeep pulled
up alongside Rizzo's truck and the driver got out and

ran shakily over to where Rizzo was standing. He was unshaven and red-eyed. His khakis were ragged and filthy and his voice had a slight tremor in it when he spoke. "You guys from the National Guard?" he said, louder than he should have. "Ha," Rizzo barked. "Jesus no. We may look it but we ain't."

"Oh." He turned away and Levine realized with a mild sense of shock that he was wearing two silver bars on each shoulder. He shook his head. "It's a little rough back there," he murmured and started back for the jeep.

"Sorry, sir," Levine called after him. And then more quietly, "God, Rizzo, did you see that?"

Rizzo laughed. "War is hell," he said ungraciously.

They sat there for half an hour more until finally the lieutenant showed up. They told him about the captain who was looking for the National Guard and gave him the newspaper's account of the hurricane. "Well, let's get moving," Pierce said. "They're bitching back there about commo."

It turned out the army had taken over McNeese State College, on the outskirts of the city, for a base of operations. It was after dark when the two trucks pulled off one of the quiet campus streets onto a huge, grassy quadrangle. "Hey," Picnic yelled at Baxter, "race you to see who gets 'em up first." They set up the 40-foot antennas and Baxter and Rizzo won. "What the hell," Levine said, "buy you a beer when we get all this junk set up." Picnic got to work on the TCC-3 and Levine started setting up AN/GRC-10. About midnight they had communications.

Baxter stuck his head in the back of the truck. "You guys owe us a beer," he said.

"You got any idea where the bars are around here?" Levine said. "You're the Joe College in the crowd," Baxter said, "you and Rizzo. You ought to be able to home right in on one."

"Yeah Nathan," Picnic said gently, looking up from the TCC-3. "You ought to feel like an old grad."

"Sure," Levine said, "sure, homecoming week. Why don't I just punch you in the mouth or something."

"Why don't you buy us a beer," Baxter said.

They found a small, collegiate-type bar a few blocks away. McNeese was holding summer session at the time and there were a few couples inside, dancing to rhythm and blues records. There was also a rack of beer mugs with people's names on them. It was that kind of a place. "Oh well," Baxter said cheerfully, "beer is beer."

"Let's sing college drinking songs," Rizzo said. Levine looked at him. "You serious?" he said.

"Personally," Baxter said, "I never could see this college crap. The way I figure nothing beats experience."

"Lout," Rizzo said, "you are in the presence of three of the army's first-rate intellectuals."

"Don't group me," Levine said quietly. "I'm a career man, is what I am."

"That's what I mean, hey Nathan," Baxter said. "You got a college diploma and you're still no better off than me, who never got past high school."

"Levine's trouble," said Rizzo, "is that he is at least the laziest bastard in the army. He doesn't want to work and therefore he is afraid to let down roots. He is a seed that casts himself on stony places, with no deepness of earth."

"And when the sun comes up," Levine smiled, "it scorches me and I wither away. Why the hell do you think I stay in the barracks so much?"

"Rizzo's right," Baxter said, "they don't come no stonier than Ft. Roach, Louisiana."

"The sun don't come any hotter, that's for damn sure," Picnic said. They sat and drank and talked till 3 in the morning. Back at the truck Picnic said, "Man, that Rizzo talks a lot." Levine folded his hands over his stomach and yawned. "Somebody's got to, I reckon," he said.

At daybreak Levine woke up to a great roar, a head-splitting clatter out in the middle of the quad. "Arrrgh," he said, holding his head in his hands, "what in the hell is that." It had stopped raining and Picnic was outside. "Look at 'em," he said. Levine stuck his head out and took a look. A hundred yards away, one by one, like giant insects, army helicopters were taking off to see what was left of Creole. "I'll be damned," Picnic said. "Last night, they were there all the time." Levine closed his eyes and settled back. "Nights get pretty dark here," he said and went back to sleep. He woke up at noon, hungry, his head throbbing. "Picnic," he groaned, "where the hell do you eat around here." Picnic snored. "Hey," Levine grabbed him by the head and shook him. "What," Picnic said. "I said I wonder if they got field kitchens or something someplace," Levine said. Rizzo climbed out of his truck and came over. "Christ you guys are lazy," he said. "We been up since ten." Out on the quad helicopters were taking off and landing with survivors. Ambulances and a swarm of medics and corpsmen were out there ready for them. Deuce-and-a-halfs and jeeps and 3/4's were parked all over the place and all sorts of army personnel, most of them in fatigues, with here and there a gleam of khaki and a flash of brass, were roaming around. "God," Levine said, "what hit this place."

"There's also newspapermen, *Life* photographers and probably a couple of newsreels around too," Rizzo said. "This is a disaster area now. Official."

"Goodo," Picnic said, blinking. "Man, look at the quail." For a summer session there did seem to be quite a few good-looking coeds roaming around among the olive drab horde. Baxter was jubilant. "I knew if I stuck around long enough at Roach," he said, "something good was bound to happen."

"Like Bourbon St. on payday night," Rizzo said.

"Don't remind me," Levine said. Then as an after-thought, "Still, here, N'Orleans, what the hell." He caught sight of a deuce-and-a-half about 20 yards away with 131st signal battalion written on the side. One fender was missing and there were dents all over it. "Hey Douglas," he yelled. A lanky redheaded PFC, sitting against one of the front wheels, looked up. "Well gaw damn," he called back. "What took you guys so long?" Levine went over. "When did you get here?" he said. "Hell," Douglas said, "they tried to send me and Steele through last night, right after it hit. Damn hurricane blew this ol' deuce-and-a-half right off the road." Levine looked at the truck. "How is it down there?" he said. "Hard to say," Douglas answered. "The only bridge over there is out. They got the engineers working their ass off to get a pontoon bridge over. From what I hear you never seen a town so screwed up. It's under maybe 8 feet of water and the only thing standing is the court-house, on account of it's concrete. And stiffs, man they got tugboats bringing 'em in and stacking them up like firewood. Stinks pretty bad."

"All right, you cheerful bastard," Levine said. "I haven't had breakfast yet."

"Man, you're gonna be living off sandwiches and coffee for a while," Douglas said. "They got all kinds of broads running around offering it to you. Sandwiches and coffee I mean. Ain't seen any of the other, not yet anyway."

"Don't worry," Levine said, "you will. We all will. We damn well better, cause I ain't losing a leave for nothing." He went back to the truck. Picnic and Rizzo were sitting on the fenders eating sandwiches and drinking coffee.

"Where did you find that," Levine said. "Some broad came around," Rizzo said. "I'll be damned," Levine said. "For once that bum dope artist was telling the truth."

"Stick around," Rizzo said. "One'll come by."

"I don't know," said Levine, "I may starve to death. My luck's been known to run that way." He indicated with his head a group of coeds and said to Rizzo – sensing there a curious empathy which had also lain dormant for a while – "It's sure been a long time."

Rizzo gave a hollow laugh. "What are you, homesick or what," he said. Levine shook his head. "Not exactly. What I mean is something like a closed circuit. Everybody on the same frequency. And after a while you forget about the rest of the spectrum and start believing that this is the only frequency that counts or is real. While outside, all up and down the land, there are these wonderful colors and x-rays and ultraviolets going on."

"Don't you think Roach is on a closed circuit too?" Rizzo said. "McNeese is not the world but Roach ain't the spectrum either."

Levine shook his head. "You draftees are all alike," he said.

"I know, I know. R.A. all the way. But all the way to what?"

A little blonde came over with a basket full of sandwiches and paper containers of coffee, and Levine said, "Just in time, honey. You have saved me from certain death." She smiled at him. "Oh you don't look so bad."

Levine took three or four sandwiches and a cup of coffee. "You either," he said, leering. "They're making St. Bernards a hell of a lot cuter than they used to."

"That's a pretty dubious compliment," she said, "but it's in better taste than any I've had today."

"What's your name, in case I get hungry again," Levine said. "I'm called little Buttercup," she answered, laughing.

"A comedian," Levine said. "Why don't you get together with Rizzo. He's a college kid. You can play Spot This Quote or something."

"Don't mind him," Rizzo said. "He's just a plowboy."

She brightened. "And how do you like plowing?" she said.

"Later," Levine said and slurped coffee.

"Later indeed," she said. "See you around the quad."

Rizzo was singing Betty Coed in an off-key tenor, a crooked smile on his face. "Shut up," Levine said, "it's not funny." "Boy you're fighting it, ain't you?" Rizzo said.

"Who's fighting?" Levine said. "Hey," Douglas yelled over, "I'm taking a jeep down to the pier. Anybody want to come along?"

"I'll stand by the circuit," Picnic said. "Go ahead," Baxter said. "I'd rather stick around where there's broads." Rizzo laughed. "I got to keep an eye on junior," he said, "he might lose his virginity." Baxter scowled. "Your next'll be your first."

Levine climbed in next to Douglas in one of the battalion jeeps and they jolted off. At the edge of the campus they hit a macadam road whose surface steadily degenerated as they got closer to the Gulf. There was not much indication that the hurricane had passed that way: only a few trees and signs down, a few roof tiles or clapboards scattered around. Douglas kept up a running commentary, mostly second-hand statistics, and Levine nodded absently. He was beginning to have a vague idea that Rizzo might not be such a Perennial Undergraduate after all – that occasionally the little sergeant did manage to get a glimpse of the truth. He was also starting to worry: to anticipate some radical change, perhaps, after three years of sand, concrete and sun. It might only be that this was the first college campus he had set foot on since graduating from CCNY – on the other hand maybe it was just time for a change. Going AWOL when he got back to Roach, or taking off on a three-day drunk might help to relieve what he was just beginning to recognize as monotony.

The pier was as crowded as the quadrangle had been, but the pace slower, more obviously ordered. The oil company tugs would bring in a bunch of corpses, the work detail would offload them, the corpsmen would spray them with embalming fluid to keep them from falling apart, another detail would load them into deuce-and-a-halfs and the deuce-and-a-halfs would cart them off. "They're keeping them in some junior high gymnasium," Douglas informed Levine, "ice all over the place. Having a hell of a time identifying them. Water screws up their faces or something." The smell of decay hung in the air, like vermouth, it seemed to Levine, after you'd been drinking it all night. The death detail worked precisely, efficiently, like an assembly line. Every once in a while one of the offloaders would turn aside to vomit, but the work flowed on smoothly. Levine and Douglas sat watching them while the sky got darker, losing more of the sun which nobody could see. An old master sergeant came over to them and leaned against the side of the jeep and they talked for a while. "I was in Korea," he said after one of the bodies had disintegrated from clumsy handling, "I can understand *guys* shooting at each other, killing each other, but this – " He shook his head. "Jesus Christ." There were brass wandering around, but none of them bothered Levine or Douglas. Despite its machine-like efficiency the operation had a certain air of informality: hardly anyone wore hats, a colonel or a major would stop to chat with the corpsmen. "Like combat," the sergeant said. "All the rules are out. Hell, who needs 'em anyway." They stayed till half past five and then drove back. "Where do you find a shower," Levine said, "or don't you." The PFC grinned. "I got a buddy took one in a sorority house last night," he said. "Damn near anyplace you can find one, I reckon."

When they got back to the trucks Levine looked in on Picnic. "Cut out," he said. "If you can find a shower someplace let me know."

"Damn, that's right," Picnic said. "It *is* July, isn't it." Levine took his place at the Angry Ten and listened to the circuit for a while; nothing much was happening. Half an hour later Picnic was back. "What the hell," he said, "Rizzo's listening over there. He wants to be R.A., why should we sweat it. What you do is you go about a block past the chapel, there's this dormitory. You can't miss it. All kinds of people going in and out."

"Thanks," Levine said, "back in five. We'll go get a beer or something." He got a clean change of skivvies and fatigues and his shaving kit out of the laundry bag and walked out into the warm heavy darkness. The copters were still landing and taking off, their head and taillights making them look like something out of a science fiction movie. Levine found the dormitory, went in, showered, shaved, changed clothes. When he got back Picnic was reading *Swamp Wench*. They went out and found another bar, noisier and thronged with a Friday night crowd. They got a glimpse of Baxter, trying to put the make on a girl whose date was already too drunk to want to fight about it. "Oh god," Levine said. Picnic looked at him. "Not to sound like Rizzo or anything," he said, "but what's the matter, Nathan? Where is the old Sgt. Bilko type soldier we used to know and love? Is the past beginning to close in or are you on the verge of undergoing an intellectual crisis or what."

Levine shrugged. "It's probably only my stomach," he said. "After all the time I've been developing and caring for this here beer belly, something like those stiffs comes along and throws it out of kilter."

"Bad, I guess," Picnic said. "Yeah," Levine said. "Let's talk about something else."

They sat and watched the college kids, each trying to look at it as something unusual and nothing they had ever been or would ever want to be part of. The blonde who called herself little Buttercup came over and said, "Spot this quote."

"I know a better game," Levine said.

"Ha, ha," the blonde said and sat down. "My date was ill," she explained, "he had to go home."

"There but for the grace of god," Picnic said.

"Been working hard?" little Buttercup asked with a bright smile. Levine leaned back and put his arm carelessly over her shoulders. "I only work hard when the end is worth it," he said, looking at her, and they tried to stare each other down for a while until he smiled with a kind of small triumph and added, "or attainable."

She raised her eyebrows. "Maybe even then you don't have to work so hard," she said.

"What are you doing tomorrow night," Levine said, "we'll find out." An adolescent-looking rebel in a cord coat came staggering up to them and flung an arm around her neck, knocking over Picnic's beer in the process. "Oh Jesus Christ," she said, "are you back?" Picnic gazed down at his soaked fatigues sadly. "What a dandy excuse for a fight," he said. "Shall we, Nathan." Baxter had been eavesdropping. "Yeah," he said, "now you're talking, Benny buddy." He swung a wild roundhouse at nobody in particular which caught Picnic on the side of the head and knocked him off the chair. "God," Levine said, looking down, "you all right Benny?" Picnic did not answer. Levine shrugged. "Come on, Baxter, let's take him back. Excuse me, little Buttercup." They picked up Picnic and carried him back to the truck.

The next morning Levine was awake at seven. He wandered around the campus for a while looking for a cup of coffee and after breakfast came to one of those spur-of-the-moment decisions which it is always fun to wonder about afterward. "Hey Rizzo," he said, shaking the sergeant. "Anybody comes looking for me, the general or the secretary of the army, tell them I'm busy, okay?" Rizzo muttered something which might have been obscene and went back to sleep.

Levine hitched a ride down to the pier on a battalion jeep and hung around for a while watching them bringing in bodies. Finally when one of the tugs had almost offloaded he sauntered down to the dock and climbed on board. No one, apparently, noticed him. There were half a dozen army personnel and as many civilians, sitting or standing, not talking; smoking or looking at the gray swamp which crawled by. They passed the pontoon bridge, which the engineers had almost completed, pushing past it into flotsam and between shattered trees. They chugged over Creole, past the top floors of the courthouse, toward the outlying farms that were still standing, which had not yet been searched. Occasionally a helicopter would chatter by overhead. The sun rose, weak through a thin overcast, heating the unstirred and reeking air over the swamp.

It was mostly this that Levine remembered afterward, the peculiar atmospheric effect of gray sun on gray swamp, the way the air felt and smelled. For ten hours they cruised around looking for dead. One they unhooked from a barbed wire fence. It hung there like a foolish balloon, a travesty; until they touched it and it popped, hissed and collapsed. They took them off roofs, out of trees, they found them floating or tangled in the debris of houses. Levine worked in silence like the others, the sun hot on his neck and face, the reek of the swamp and the corpses in his lungs, letting it all happen, now exactly unwilling to think about it nor quite unable; but realizing somehow that the situation did not require thought or rationalization. He was picking up stiffs. That was what he was doing. When the tug pulled in around six to offload bodies, Levine walked off as carelessly as he had climbed aboard. He hopped a deuce-and-a-half back to the quadrangle, sitting in back dirty and exhausted and sick at his own smell. He got clean clothing out of the truck, disregarding Picnic, who was almost finished with *Swamp Wench* and who had started to say something but had thought better of it, walked to the dormitory and stood under the shower for a long time, thinking it was like rain, summer and spring rain, all the times he had ever been rained on, and when he came out of the dormitory in a clean uniform he noticed it was dark again.

Back at the truck he dug the blue baseball cap out of his bag and put it on. "Going formal," Picnic said. "What's up?"

"Date," Levine said.

"Fine," Picnic said, "I like to see young people get together. It's real exciting."

Levine looked at him, dead serious. "No," he said. "No, I think 'sheer momentum' is better."

He went over to Rizzo's truck and swiped a pack of cigarettes and a De Nobili cigar from Rizzo, who was sleeping. As he was leaving the sergeant opened one eye. "Why it's good old reliable Nathan," he said. "Go to sleep, Rizzo," Levine said. He started walking, hands in his pockets, whistling, heading in the general direction of the bar he had been in the night before. There were no stars and the air felt like rain. He walked through the streetlit shadows of big ugly pines, listening to the voices of girls, the purr of cars, wondering what the hell he was doing here when he should be back at Roach, having a pretty good idea that when he got back to Roach he would start wondering what the hell he was doing there, and that maybe wherever he went from now on he would be wondering this. He had a momentary, ludicrous vision of himself, Lardass Levine the Wandering Jew, debating on weekday evenings in strange and nameless towns with other Wandering Jews the essential problems of identity – not of the self so much as an identity of place and what right you really had to be anyplace. He got to the bar and went inside and there was little Buttercup waiting for him.

"I got us a car," she smiled. He was aware all at once that she had a slight Rebel accent. "Hey," he said, "what y'all drinking?"

"Tom Collins," she said. Levine drank scotch. Her face got serious. "Is it bad out there?" she said. "Pretty bad," Levine said. She smiled again, brightly. "At least it didn't do anything to the college."

"It sure did something to Creole," Levine said.

"Well, Creole," she said. Levine looked at her.

"You mean better them than the college," he said.

"Why sure," she grinned. He tapped his fingers on the table. "Say 'out'," he said.

"Oot," she said.

"Ah," said Levine. They drank and talked for a while, mostly on collegiate topics, until finally Levine expressed a desire to see what the bayou country looked like under a sky without stars. They left and he drove, toward the Gulf, the night muffled around them. She sat close to him, aroused, impatient, touching him. He was quiet until she indicated a dirt road which led into the swamp. "In here," she whispered, "there's a cabin."

"I was beginning to wonder," he said. Around them thousands of frogs chanted to themselves in an inexplicable set of chord changes, to the glory of certain ambiguous principles. Mangrove and moss closed in on them. They drove for a mile until they came to a dilapidated building, out in the boondocks of nowhere. It turned out there was a mattress inside. "It's not much," she said between breaths, "but it's home." She quivered against him in the dark. He found Rizzo's stogie and lit up; her face trembled in the light of the flame and there was in her eyes something that might have been a dismayed and delayed acknowledgement that what was hazarding this particular plowboy was deeper than any problem of seasonal change or doubtful fertility, precisely as he had recognized earlier that her capacity to give involved nothing over or above the list of enumerated wares: scissors, watches, knives, ribands, laces; and therefore he assumed toward her that same nonchalant compassion which he felt for the heroines of sex novels, or for the burned out but impotent good guy rancher in a western. He let her undress apart from him; until, standing there in nothing but T-shirt and baseball cap, puffing placidly on the stogie he heard her from the mattress, whimpering.

Around them frogs intoned a savage chorus, gradually it seemed to them – spasmodic as they were, blinded yet curiously aware of this as little more than an entwining of little fingers, a touching of beer mugs, a *McCall's* togetherness – working itself into a pedal bass for a virtuoso duet of small breathings, cries; he puffing occasionally at the cigar throughout the performance, the ball cap tilted carelessly, she evoking a casually protective feeling, a never totally violated Pasiphae; until at last, having subsided, assailed still by stupid frog cries they lay not touching. "In the midst of great death," Levine said, "the little death." And later, "Ha. It sounds like a caption in *Life*. In the midst of *Life*. We are in death. Oh god."

They drove back and at the truck Levine said, "See you around the quad." She smiled weakly. "Come on around and visit me when you get out," she said and drove away. Picnic and Baxter were playing blackjack under the headlights. "Hey Levine," Baxter said, "I got laid tonight."

"Ah," Levine said. "Congratulations."

The next day the lieutenant came around and said, "You can take that leave, Levine, if you want. Everything's set up now. You're just an extra body."

Levine shrugged. "All right," he said. It was raining. Back at the truck Picnic said, "Jesus Christ I hate rain."

"You and Hemingway," Rizzo said. "Funny, ain't it. T. S. Eliot likes rain."

Levine slung his bag over one shoulder. "Rain is pretty weird that way," he said. "It can stir dull roots; it can rip them up, wash them away. I will think of you boys as I bask in the sun down in N'Orleans, up here up to your ass in water."

"So go," Picnic said, "go already."

"By the way," Rizzo said, "Pierce wanted you yesterday but I gave him some crap about finding a part for the TCC. It took me a while though to figure out where it was you'd gone." "Christ, let me in on it," Levine said quietly. "I'm still trying to figure it out," Rizzo grinned. "See you guys," Levine said. He bummed a ride off a deuce-and-a-half that was heading back to Roach. A couple of miles out of town the PFC who was driving said, "Damn, it'll almost be a relief to get back."

"Back?" Levine said. "Oh, yeah, I guess so." He watched the windshield wipers pushing the rain away, listened to the rain slashing on the roof. After a while he fell asleep.

LOW-LANDS

AT HALF past five in the afternoon Dennis Flange was still entertaining the garbage man. The garbage man's name was Rocco Squarcione, and around nine that morning, directly after finishing his route, he had arrived at the Flange residence with an orange peel still clinging to his dungaree shirt and a gallon of home-made muscatel dangling from a large fist speckled with coffee grounds. "Hey *sfacim'*," he bellowed from the living room. "I got wine. Come on down."

"Fine," Flange yelled back, deciding not to go to work after all. He called up Wasp and Winsome, Attorneys at Law, and got somebody's secretary. "Flange," he said: "no." She began to object. "Later," he said, hung up and sat with Rocco for the rest of the day drinking muscatel and listening to a $1,000 stereo outfit that Cindy had made him buy but which she had never used, to Flange's recollection, for anything but a place to put hors d'oeuvre dishes or cocktail trays. Cindy was Mrs. Flange and need-less to say she did not dig this muscatel business. She did

not dig Rocco Squarcione either. Or as a matter of fact
any of her husband's friends. "You keep that weird crew
down in the rumpus room," she would yell, brandishing
a cocktail shaker. "You are a damned ASPCA, is what
you are. I doubt if even they would take some of the
animals you bring home." What Flange should have answered but didn't was something like, "Rocco Squarcione
is not an animal, he is a garbage man with a fondness,
among other things, for Vivaldi." It was Vivaldi they
were listening to now, Sixth Concerto for Violin, sub-
titled *Il Piacere,* while Cindy stomped around upstairs.
Flange got the impression she was throwing things. He
wondered every once in a while what life would be like
without a second story and how it was people managed
to get along in ranch-style or split-level houses without
running amok once a year or so. The Flange abode perched
on a cliff overlooking the Sound. It had been built vaguely
to resemble an English cottage back in the '20's by an
Episcopal minister who ran bootleg stuff in from Canada
on the side. It seemed everyone living on the north shore
of Long Island at the time was engaged in some kind of
smuggling, because there are all kinds of little spits and
bays, necks and inlets which the Feds still have no idea
exist. The minister must have taken a romantic attitude
toward the whole business: the house rose in a big mossy
tumulus out of the earth, its color that of one of the
shaggier prehistoric beasts. Inside were priest-holes and
concealed passageways and oddly angled rooms; and in
the cellar, leading from the rumpus room, innumerable
tunnels, which writhed away radically like the tentacles of
a spastic octopus into dead ends, storm drains, abandoned
sewers and occasionally a secret wine cellar. Dennis and
Cindy Flange had lived in this curious moss-thatched,
almost organic mound for the seven years of their marriage

and in this time Flange at least had come to feel attached
to the place by an umbilical cord woven of lichen and
sedge, furze and gorse; he called it his womb with a view
and in their now infrequent moments of tenderness he
would sing Cindy the Noel Coward song, half as an
attempt to recall the first few months they were together,
half as a love song for the house:

> *"We'll be as happy and contented*
> *As birds upon a tree,*
> *High above the mountains and sea . . ."*

However Noel Coward songs often bear little relevance
to reality – if Flange hadn't known this before he soon
found it out – and if after seven years it turned out he
was less a bird upon a tree than a mole within a burrow
it was Cindy more than the house who was responsible.
His analyst, a crazed and boozy wetback named Geronimo
Diaz, had, of course, a great deal to say about this. For
fifty minutes every week Flange would be screamed at
over martinis about his mom. The fact that the money
spent on these sessions could have bought every auto-
mobile, pedigreed dog and woman on the stretch of
Park Avenue visible from the doctor's office window
disturbed Flange less than the dim suspicion he was
somehow being cheated: it may have been that he considered himself a legitimate child of his generation,
and, Freud having been mother's milk for that generation,
he felt he was learning nothing new. But he would
occasionally be caught, nights when snow drove down
out of Connecticut, across the Sound, to lash at the
bedroom window and remind him that he was lying in
the foetal position after all: he would be caught red-
handed at Molemanship, which is less a behavior pattern

than a state of mind in which one does not hear the snow at all, and the snorings of one's wife are as the drool and trickle of amniotic fluid somewhere outside the blankets, and even the secret cadences of one's pulse become mere echoes of the house's heartbeat.

Geronimo Diaz was clearly insane; but it was a wonderful, random sort of madness which conformed to no known model or pattern, an irresponsible plasma of delusion he floated in, utterly convinced, for example, that he was Paganini and had sold his soul to the devil. He kept a priceless Stradivarius in his desk, and to prove to Flange that this hallucination was fact he would saw away on the strings, producing horribly raucous noises, throw down the bow finally and say, "You see. Ever since I made that deal I haven't been able to play a note." And spend whole sessions reading aloud to himself out of random-number tables or the Ebbinghaus nonsense-syllable lists, ignoring everything that Flange would be trying to tell him. Those sessions were impossible: counterpointed against confessions of clumsy adolescent sex play would come this incessant "ZAP. MOG. FUD. NAF. VOB," and every once in a while the clink and gurgle of the martini shaker. But Flange went back again, he kept going back; realizing perhaps that if he were subjected for the rest of his life to nothing but the relentless rationality of that womb and that wife, he would never make it, and that Geronimo's lunacy was about all he had to keep him going. And the martinis were free.

Besides his analyst Flange had only one other consolation: the sea. Or Long Island Sound, which at times was close enough to the brawling gray image he remembered. He had read or heard somewhere in his pre-adolescence that the sea was a woman, and the metaphor had enslaved him and largely determined what he became from that moment. It had meant, for one thing, communications officer for three years on a destroyer which did nothing for the duration but run hourglass-shaped barrier patrols, day and night and for everybody but Flange too long, off the Korean coast. It had meant, when he finally got out and dragged Cindy from her mother's flat in Jackson Heights to find a home near the sea, this large half-earthen mass at the top of a cliff. Geronimo had pointed out, rather pedantically, that since all life had started from protozoa who lived in the sea, and since, as life forms had grown more complicated, sea water had begun to serve the function of blood until eventually corpuscles and a lot of other junk were added to produce the red stuff we know today; since this was true, the sea was quite literally in our blood, and more important, the sea – rather than, as is popularly held, the earth – is the true mother image for us all. At this point Flange had attempted to brain his psychiatrist with the Stradivarius. "But you said yourself the sea was a woman," protested Geronimo, leaping up on the desk. *"Chinga tu madre,"* roared Flange, enraged. "Aha," Geronimo beamed, "you see."

So that whether it crashed, moaned or merely slopped around down there a hundred feet below his bedroom window, the sea was with Flange in his hours of need, which were getting to be more and more frequent; a repetition in miniature of that Pacific whose unimaginable heavings kept his memory at a constant 30° list. If the goddess Fortune controls everything this side of the moon then there must be, he felt, a curious and tender dominion or swing about the Pacific, which some say is the chasm the moon left when it tore loose from the earth. A peculiar double of his was sole inhabitant in this tilt of memory: Fortune's elf child and disinherited darling, young and randy and more a Jolly Jack Tar than anyone human could conceivably be; thews and chin taut against a sixty-knot gale with a well-broken-in briar clenched in the bright defiant teeth; standing OOD on the bridge through the midwatch with only a dozing quartermaster and a faithful helmsman and a sewer-mouthed radar crew and a red-dog game in the sonar shack, along with the ripped-off exile moon and its track on the ocean for company. Although what the moon would be doing out during a sixty-knot gale was open to question. But that was the way he remembered it: there he had been, Dennis Flange in his prime, without the current signs of incipient middle age; and, most important, as far away from Jackson Heights as anybody can get, though he wrote to Cindy every other night. That was when the marriage too had been in its prime; but now it was getting a slight beer belly and its hair was beginning to fall out, and Flange was still wondering vaguely why this ever should have happened even as Vivaldi discoursed on pleasure and Rocco Squarcione gargled his muscatel.

The doorbell rang in the middle of the second movement and Cindy came suddenly roaring downstairs like a small blond terrier to answer it, managing to scowl at Flange and Rocco before she opened the door. Standing there when she opened it was what looked like an ape in a naval uniform, squat and leering. She stared level at him, aghast. "No," she wailed. "You ugly bastard."

"Who is it," Flange said.

"It's Pig Bodine, is who it is," Cindy said, appalled. "After seven years your big gaping idiot buddy Pig Bodine."

"Hi babe," Pig Bodine said.

"Old goodbuddy," Flange yelled, leaping up. "Come in and drink some wine. Rocco, it's Pig Bodine. I told you about Pig."

"Oh no," Cindy said, barring the door. Flange, afflicted by marriage, had personal warning signals like those afflicted by epilepsy. He sensed one now. "No," his wife growled. "Out. Go. Get out. You. Move."

"Me," Flange said.

"You," Cindy said. "You, Rocco and Pig. The three musketeers. Get out."

"Wha," Flange said. They had been through this before. It ended up the same way every time: out in the yard was this abandoned police booth which the Nassau County cops had used once upon a time to check on speeders, out on Route 25A. It had so captivated Cindy that she had finally had it carted home, and planted ivy around it and hung Mondrians inside and this was where Flange slept whenever they had a fight. The funny thing was it made little difference to his sense of snugness: the booth was womblike as could be and Mondrian and Cindy, he suspected, were brother and sister under the skin, both austere and logical.

"All right," he said, "I'll take a blanket and go out and sleep in the booth, hey."

"No," Cindy said. "Out is what I said and out is where you are going. Of my life, is what I mean. Booze all day with the garbage man is pretty bad but Pig Bodine is enough and enough is too much."

"Jeez babe," Pig put in, "I figured you'd forgotten about all that. Look at your husband. He's glad to see me." Pig had hit the Manhasset station some time between five and six, in the middle of the commuter rush. He was swept out of the train, propelled by briefcases and folded copies of the *Times,* and up to the parking lot, where he stole a '51 MG and set out to find Flange, who had been his division officer during the Korean conflict. He was nine days AWOL from the minesweeper *Immaculate,* docked in Norfolk, and wanted to see how his old buddy was making out. The last time Cindy had seen him was in Norfolk, on the night of her wedding. Just before his ship had been reassigned to the Seventh Fleet, Flange had managed to swing thirty days' leave, which he and Cindy were going to use for a honeymoon. Only Pig, upset because the enlisted men had not had a chance to give Flange a bachelor party, descended with five or six friends on the reception at the NOB officers' club, disguised as boot ensigns, and dragged Flange off to East Main Street to have a few beers. This "few beers" was sort of a rough estimate. Two weeks later Cindy received a telegram from Cedar Rapids, Iowa. It was from Flange and he was broke and horribly hung over. Cindy thought about this for two days and finally wired him bus fare home, with the stipulation that she never set eyes on Pig again. She had not. Not until now. But her feeling that Pig was the most loathsome creature in the world had continued unabated for seven years, and now she was ready to prove it. "Out that door," she said, pointing, "over the hill and far away. Or over the cliff, I don't care. You and your wino friend and that foul ape in the sailor suit. Begone."

Flange scratched his head and blinked at her for a minute or so. No. He figured not. Maybe if they had had kids. . . . He considered it a fine and lovely irony that the navy had made him a competent communications officer. "Well," he said slowly, "all right, I reckon."

"You can have the Volkswagen," Cindy said, "and take some shaving gear and a clean shirt."

"No," Flange said, opening the door for Rocco, who had been hulking in the background with the wine bottle, "no, I'll ride with Rocco in the truck." Cindy shrugged. "And grow a beard," he added vaguely. They left the house – Pig bewildered, Rocco singing to himself and

Flange beginning to feel the first faint tendrils of nausea creeping up to surround his stomach – and piled into the truck and roared off. Flange, looking back, could see his wife standing in the doorway watching them. They pulled out of the drive and on to a narrow macadam road. "Where to," Rocco said.

"I don't know," Flange said. "Maybe I'll go into New York and find a hotel or something. You might as well drop me off at the station. You got any place to stay, hey Pig?"

"I could of slept in the MG," Pig said, "but the fuzz probably know about it by now."

"I tell you what," Rocco said. "I got to go to the dump anyway and get rid of this load. I got this buddy there who's sort of a watchman. He lives there. He has all kinds of room. You could stay there."

"Sure," Flange said. "Why not." It suited his mood. They headed south, into that part of the Island which is nothing but housing developments and shopping centers and various small, light-industrial factories and after half an hour they pulled in to the town dump. "It's closed," Rocco said, "but he'll open up." He turned down a dirt road running behind an incinerator with adobe walls and a tiled roof, which had been designed and built back in the '30's by some mad WPA architect, and which looked like a Mexican hacienda with smokestacks. They jolted along for about a hundred yards and came to a gate. "Bolingbroke," Rocco yelled. "Let me in. I got wine."

"All right man," a voice answered out of the dusk. A minute later a fat Negro with a pork-pie hat appeared in the headlight beams, unlocked the gate and hopped on the running board. They started down a long spiraling road into the dump. "This here is Bolingbroke," Rocco said. "He'll put you up." They were descending in a long

[*63*]

wide curve. It seemed to Flange that they must be heading for the center of the spiral, the low point. "These guys need some place to sleep?" Bolingbroke said. Rocco explained the problem. Bolingbroke nodded sympathetically. "Wife is a nuisance sometimes," he said. "I got three or four scattered around the country and glad to be rid of them all. Somehow you never seem to learn."

The dump was roughly square, half a mile on each side, sunk fifty feet below the streets of the sprawling housing development which surrounded it. All day long, Rocco said, two D-8 bulldozers would bury the refuse under fill which was brought in from the north shore, and which raised the level of that floor a tiny fraction of an inch every day. It was this peculiar quality of fatedness which struck Flange as he gazed off into the half-light while Rocco dumped the load: this thought that one day, perhaps fifty years from now, perhaps more, there would no longer be any hole: the bottom would be level with the streets of the development, and houses would be built on it too. As if some maddeningly slow elevator were carrying you toward a known level to confer with some inevitable face on matters which had already been decided. But something else too: here at the end of the spiral he felt haunted by yet another correspondence, and could not place it until searching back he came to the music and words of a song. You would hardly think, in a modern-day navy of jet planes, missiles and nuclear submarines, that anyone still sang sea chanteys or ballads; but Flange remembered a Filipino steward named Delgado who used to come up to the radio shack late at night with a guitar and sit and sing them for hours. There are many ways of telling a sea story, but perhaps because of the music and because the words had nothing to do with personal legend, Delgado's way seemed tinged with truth of a special order. Despite even the traditional ballads' being lies or at best tall tales just as surely as the ones talked not sung over coffee in the boatswain's locker or during payday-stakes poker in the mess hall or while sitting on a depth charge out on the fantail waiting for the evening's movie to replace one yarn with another more palpable. But the steward preferred to sing and Flange respected that. And his favorite was a song which went:

> *A ship I have got in the North Country*
> *And she goes by the name of the* Golden Vanity,
> *O, I fear she will be taken by a Spanish Gal-la-lee,*
> *As she sails by the Low-lands low.*

It is very easy to be pedantic and say that Low-lands refers to the southern and eastern parts of Scotland; the ballad was certainly of Scottish origin, but it always called up a weird irrational association for Flange. Anyone who has looked at the open sea under a special kind of illumination or in a mood conducive to metaphor will tell you of the curious illusion that the ocean, despite its movement, has a certain solidity; it becomes a gray or glaucous desert, a waste land which stretches away to the horizon, and all you would have to do would be to step over the lifelines to walk away over its surface; if you carried a tent and enough provisions you could journey from city to city that way. Geronimo regarded this as a bizarre variation on the Messiah complex, and advised Flange in a fatherly way not to try it, ever; but for Flange that immense clouded-glass plain was a kind of low-land which almost demanded a single human figure striding across it for completeness; any arrival at sea level was like finding a minimum and dimensionless point, a unique crossing of parallel and meridian, an assurance of perfect, passionless uniformity; just as in the spiraling descent of Rocco's truck he had felt that this spot at which they finally came to rest was the dead center, the single point which implied an entire low country. Whenever he was away from Cindy and could think he would picture his life as a surface in the process of change, much as the floor of the dump was in transition: from concavity or inclosure to perhaps a flatness like the one he stood in now. What he worried about was any eventual convexity, a shrinking, it might be, of the planet itself to some palpable curvature of whatever he would be standing on, so that he would be left sticking out like a projected radius, unsheltered and reeling across the empty lunes of his tiny sphere.

Rocco left them with another gallon of muscatel which he had found under the seat and went bouncing and snarling away into the gathering darkness. Bolingbroke unscrewed the cap and drank. They passed the bottle around and Bolingbroke said, "Come on, we'll find mattresses." He led them up a slope, around a tall tower of bank run, past half an acre of abandoned refrigerators, bicycles, baby carriages, washing machines, sinks, toilets, bedsprings, TV sets, pots and pans and stoves and air-conditioners and finally over a dune to where the mattresses were. "Biggest bed in the world," Bolingbroke said. "Take your pick." There must have been thousands of mattresses. Flange found a three-quarter-width inner-spring and Pig, who would probably never get accustomed to civilian life, selected a pallet about two inches thick and three feet wide. "I wouldn't feel comfortable otherwise," Pig said.

"Hurry up," Bolingbroke called softly, nervously. He had climbed to the top of the dune and was looking back in the direction they had come. "Hurry. It's almost dark."

"What's wrong," Flange said, lugging the mattress up the slope to stand next to him and peer out over the junk pile. "You have prowlers at night?"

"Something like that," Bolingbroke said, uncomfortable. "Come on." They trudged back, retracing their steps, no one speaking. At the place where the truck had stopped they angled off to the left. Above them towered the incinerator, its stacks tall and black against the last sky-glow. The three entered a narrow ravine which had garbage scattered twenty feet up its sides. Flange got the feeling that this dump was like an island or enclave in the dreary country around it, a discrete kingdom with Bolingbroke its uncontested ruler. The ravine ran on for a hundred yards, steep-sided and tortuous, until at length it opened out on a small valley completely filled with cast-off rubber tires from cars, trucks, tractors and airplanes; and in the center on a slight eminence stood Bolingbroke's shack, jury-rigged out of tar paper and refrigerator sides and haphazardly acquired wooden beams and pipes and shingles. "Home," Bolingbroke said. "Now we play follow the leader." It was like running a maze. Sometimes the stacks of tires were twice as high as Flange, threatening to topple at the slightest jar. The smell of rubber was strong in the air. "Be careful with them mattresses," Bolingbroke whispered, "don't step out of line. I got booby traps set up."

"For what," Pig said, but Bolingbroke either had not heard or was ignoring the question. They reached the shack and Bolingbroke unlocked the door, which was made from the side of a heavy packing case and was secured by a large padlock. Inside was absolute blackness. There were no windows. Bolingbroke lit a kerosene lamp and in the flickering yellow light Flange could see the walls covered with photographs clipped out of every publication, it seemed, put out since the Depression.

[*67*]

A brightly colored pin-up of Brigitte Bardot was flanked by newspaper photos of the Duke of Windsor making his abdication speech and the *Hindenburg* going up in flames. There were Ruby Keeler and Hoover and MacArthur. Jack Sharkey, Whirlaway, Lauren Bacall and God knew how many others in a rogues' gallery of faded sensation fragile as tabloid paper, blurred as the common humanity of a nine-day wonder.

Bolingbroke bolted the door. They threw down their bedding and sat, and drank wine. Outside a small wind had risen, which rattled the flaps of tar paper and blundered baffled and turbulent into and around the jutting corners and irregular angles of the shack. Somehow they started telling sea stories. Pig told about how he and a sonarman named Feeny had stolen a horse-drawn taxi in Barcelona. It turned out neither of them knew anything about horses and they wound up driving full tilt off the end of Fleet Landing, pursued by at least a platoon of Shore Patrolmen. While they were floundering around in the water it occurred to them that this would be a good time to swim out to the carrier *Intrepid* and stomp hell out of a few airedales. They would have made it had it not been for the *Intrepid*'s motor launch, which caught up with them a few hundred yards out. Feeny managed to throw the coxswain and the bow hook over the side before some wise-assed ensign with a .45 stopped all the fun by shooting Feeny through the shoulder. Flange told about how one spring weekend back in college he and two comrades had swiped a female cadaver from the local morgue. They took it up to Flange's fraternity about three in the morning and deposited it next to the president of the house, who was lying passed out on his bed. Next morning bright and early all the brothers able to ambulate marched *en masse* to the president's room and began

[*68*]

banging on the door. "Yes, just a minute," a voice groaned from inside, "I'll be right with. Oh. Oh, my god." "What's the matter, Vincent?" somebody called. "You got a broad in there?" And they all laughed good-naturedly. About fifteen minutes later Vincent, ashen and trembling, opened up and they all trooped in noisily. They looked under the bed and moved the furniture around and opened the closet, but no corpse. Puzzled, they began pulling out dresser drawers, when suddenly there was a piercing scream from outside. They rushed to the window and looked down. A coed had fainted in the street. It turned out Vincent had knotted together his three best neckties and hung the body outside the window. Pig shook his head. "Wait a minute," he said. "I thought you were gonna tell a sea story." By this time they had killed the gallon. Bolingbroke produced a jug of home-made Chianti from under his bed. "I would have," Flange said, "only I couldn't think of any offhand." But the real reason he knew and could not say was that if you are Dennis Flange and if the sea's tides are the same that not only wash along your veins but also billow through your fantasies then it is all right to listen to but not to tell stories about that sea, because you and the truth of a true lie were thrown sometime way back into a curious contiguity and as long as you are passive you can remain aware of the truth's extent but the minute you became active you are somehow, if not violating a convention outright, at least screwing up the perspective of things, much as anyone observing subatomic particles changes the works, data and odds, by the act of observing. So he had told the other instead, at random. Or apparently so. He wondered what Geronimo would say.

Bolingbroke, however, had a sea story. He had spent some time bouncing around from port to port on a variety of merchantmen, all vaguely disreputable. He had spent two months right after the first war on the beach in Caracas with a friend named Sabbarese. They had jumped a freighter called the *Deirdre O'Toole,* sailing under Panamanian registry – Bolingbroke apologized for this detail, but he insisted it was true: back then you could register anything, a rowboat, a seagoing whorehouse, a battleship, anything that floated, in Panama – to escape from Porcaccio the first mate, who had delusions of grandeur. Three days out from Port-au-Prince Porcaccio had stormed into the captain's cabin with a Very pistol and threatened to turn the captain into a human flare unless the ship were turned around and headed for Cuba. It seems there were several cases of rifles and other light armament down in the hold, all destined for a gang of banana pickers in Guatemala who had recently unionized and desired to abolish the local American sphere of influence. It was Porcaccio's intention to take over the ship and invade Cuba and claim the island for Italy, to whom it rightfully belonged, since Columbus had discovered it. For his mutiny he had assembled two Chinese wipers and a deck hand subject to epileptic fits. The captain laughed and invited Porcaccio in for a drink. Two days later they came staggering out on deck, drunk, arms flung about each other's shoulders; neither had had any sleep in the intervening period. The ship had run into a heavy squall; all hands were running around securing booms and shifting cargo, and in the confusion the captain somehow got washed over the side. Porcaccio thus became master of the *Deirdre O'Toole.* The liquor supply had run out, however, so Porcaccio decided to head for Caracas and replenish. He promised the crew a jeroboam of champagne each the day Havana was captured. Bolingbroke and Sabbarese were not about to invade Cuba. As soon as the ship docked in Caracas they went over the hill and lived off the proceeds of a barmaid, an Armenian refugee named Zenobia, sleeping with her on alternate nights, for two months. Finally something – whether homesickness for the sea or an attack of conscience or the violent and unpredictable temper of their patroness Bolingbroke had never quite decided – prompted them to visit the Italian consul and give themselves up. The consul was most understanding. He put them on an Italian merchantman bound for Genoa and they shoveled coal as if into the fires of hell all the way across the Atlantic.

By this time it was late and everybody was loaded. Bolingbroke yawned. "Good night, man," he said. "I got to be up bright and early. You hear any strange noises don't sweat it. That's a strong bolt."

"Wha," Pig said. "Who's gonna get in?" Flange began to feel uneasy.

"Nobody," Bolingbroke said, "only them. They try to get in every once in a while. But they ain't yet. And there's a hunk of pipe you can use if they do." He put out the lamp and stumbled over to his bed.

"Yeah," Pig said, "but who?"

"The gypsies," Bolingbroke yawned. His voice was drowsing off into sleep. "They live here. Here in the dump. Only come out at night." He fell silent and after a while began to snore.

Flange shrugged. What the hell. All right, there were gypsies around. He remembered back in his childhood thet they used to camp out on the deserted areas of beach along the north shore. He thought by now they had all gone; somehow he was glad they had not. It suited some half-felt sense of fitness; it was right that there should be gypsies living in the dump, just as he had been able to believe in the rightness of Bolingbroke's sea, its ability

[*71*]

to encompass and be the sustaining plasma or medium for horse-drawn taxis and Porcaccios. Not to mention that young, rogue male Flange, from whom he occasionally felt the Flange of today had suffered a sea change into something not so rare or strange. He drifted into a light, uneasy sleep, flanked by the contrapuntal snorings of Bolingbroke and Pig Bodine.

How long he slept was uncertain; he awoke in that total darkness with only the visceral time sense of its being two or three in the morning, or at least a desolate hour somehow not intended for human perception, but rather belonging to cats, owls and peepers and whatever else make noises in the night. Outside the wind was still blowing; he searched it for the sound he knew had awakened him. For a full minute there was nothing, then at last it came. A girl's voice, riding on the wind.

"Anglo," it said, "Anglo with the gold hair. Come out. Come out by the secret path and find me."

"Wha," Flange said. He shook Pig. "Hey buddy," he said, "there's a broad out there."

Pig opened one unfocused eye. "Great," he mumbled. "Bring her in and let me have seconds."

"No," said Flange, "what I mean is, this must be one of the gypsies Bolingbroke was talking about."

Pig snored. Flange groped his way over to Bolingbroke. "Hey man," he said, "she's out there." Bolingbroke did not respond. Flange shook harder. "She's *out* there," he repeated, starting to feel panicked. Bolingbroke rolled over and said something unintelligible. Flange threw up his hands. "Wha," he said.

"Anglo," the girl called insistently, "come to me. Come find me or I shall go away forever. Come out, tall Anglo with the gold hair and the shining teeth."

"Hey," Flange said to nobody in particular. "That's me, ain't it." Not quite, it occurred to him immediately. Closer to his *Doppelgänger,* that sea-dog of the lusty, dark Pacific days. He kicked Pig. "She wants me to come out," he said. "What do I do, hey."

Pig opened both eyes. "Sir," he said, "I recommend that you go out and obtain a sitrep. And if she's any good, like I say, bring her back in and let the enlisted men have a go at it."

"Aye, aye," Flange said vaguely. He made his way to the door, slid back the bolt and stepped outside. "O Anglo," he heard the voice, "you have come. Follow me."

"All right," Flange said. He began weaving his way out through the stacks of tires, praying that he wouldn't set off one of Bolingbroke's booby traps. Miraculously, he made it almost to open ground before anything went wrong. He was not exactly sure that he had misstepped but realized, suddenly, that he had goofed somehow, and looked up just in time to see a huge stack of snow tires sway and lurch, hanging for a moment against the stars before they toppled over on him, and this was the last thing he remembered for a while.

He awoke to cool fingers on his forehead and a coaxing voice: "Wake up, Anglo. Open your eyes. You're all right." He opened his eyes and saw her, the girl, her face, floating wide-eyed and anxious over him, and the stars caught in her hair. He was lying at the entrance to the ravine. "Come," she smiled. "Get up."

"Sure," Flange said. He had a headache. He was throbbing all over. He finally managed to get to his feet, and it was only then that he had a good look at her. In the starlight she was exquisite: she wore a dark dress, her legs and arms were bare, slim, the neck arching and delicate, her figure so slender it was almost a shadow.

Dark hair floated around her face and down her back like a black nebula; eyes enormous, nose retroussé, short upper lip, good teeth, nice chin. She was a dream, this girl, an angel. She was also roughly three and a half feet tall. Flange scratched his head. "How do you do," he said. "My name is Dennis Flange. Thank you for rescuing me."

"I am Nerissa," she said, gazing up at him.

He had no idea what to say to her next. The conversational possibilities were suddenly limited. Though they might, it occurred to him insanely, discuss the Midget Problem or something.

She took his hand. "Come," she said. She pulled him after her into the ravine. "Where we going," Flange said. "To my home," she answered. "It will be dawn soon." Flange thought about this. "Well wait a minute hey," he said. "What about my buddies back there. I'm abusing Bolingbroke's hospitality." She did not answer; he shrugged. What the hell. She led him through the ravine and up the slope. On top of the pinnacle of bank run stood a human figure, watching them. Other shapes hovered and flitted in the darkness; from somewhere came the sound of guitar music, and singing, and a fight in progress. They entered the junk pile he had passed before on the way to get a mattress, and they began picking their path through a cast-off chaos of starlit metal and porcelain. Finally she stopped at a General Electric refrigerator which lay on its back, and opened the door. "I hope you'll be able to fit," she said, climbed in and disappeared. Oh Christ, Flange thought, I've been putting on weight, haven't I. He climbed in; the back of the refrigerator was missing. "Shut the door after you," she called from somewhere below, and he obeyed trance-like. A beam of light shot up, probably from a flashlight she was holding, to show him the way. He had not realized that the junk pile ran to such a depth. There were some tight squeezes, but he managed to worm his way between, around and down through various loosely stacked household appliances for about thirty feet until he reached the opening of a forty-eight-inch concrete pipe. She was there waiting for him. "From here on it is easier," she said. He crawled, she walked down a gentle incline which must have run for a quarter of a mile. In the wavering beam of the flashlight, between flickering shadows, he could see that there were other tunnels which led off from this one. She noticed his curiosity. "It took them a long time," she said and told him how the entire dump had been laced with a network of tunnels and rooms back in the '30's by a terrorist group called the Sons of the Red Apocalypse, by way of making ready for the revolution. Only the Feds had rounded them all up, and a year or so later the gypsies had moved in.

They reached a dead end finally, with a small door set in the gravelly soil. She opened it and they entered. She lit candles, whose flames revealed a room hung with arrases and paintings, an immense double bed with silk sheets, an armoire, a table, a refrigerator. Flange had all kinds of questions. She told him about the air supply, and the drainage and the plumbing and the power line that had been run in without Long Island Lighting's ever suspecting; about the truck which Bolingbroke used in the daytime and which they drove out at night to steal food and supplies; about Bolingbroke's half-superstitious fear of them and his reluctance to inform anyone in authority about all this lest he be accused of alcoholism or worse and lose his job.

It occurred to Flange that there had been a gray furry rat sitting on the bed for some time, peering at them inquisitively. "Hey," he said, "there is a rat over there on the bed."

"Her name is Hyacinth," Nerissa said. "Before you came she was my only friend." Hyacinth blinked noncommittally. "That's nice," Flange said, reaching over to pet the rat. She squealed and backed away. "She is shy," Nerissa said. "She will make friends with you. Give her time."

"Ha," Flange said, "that reminds me. How long do you expect me to stay here? Why did you bring me?"

"The old woman with the eye patch who is called Violetta read my fortune many years ago," Nerissa said. "She told me a tall Anglo would be my husband and he would have bright hair and strong arms and – "

"Of course," Flange said, "yes. But us Anglos all look like that. There are all kinds of Anglos roaming around who are tall and blond."

She pouted; tears began. "You do not want me for your wife."

"Well," Flange said, embarrassed, "what it is is, I already have a wife, I'm married, is what I mean."

She looked for a moment as if she had been stabbed, then began to bawl violently.

"All I said was I was married," Flange protested. "I didn't say I enjoy it particularly."

"Please do not be angry with me, Dennis," she wailed. "Do not leave me. Say you will stay."

Flange thought about this for a while. His silence was suddenly broken by the rat Hyacinth who did a backward somersault on the bed and began to thrash around violently. With a sharp pitying gasp the girl picked up the rat, held it against her breast and began to stroke it, croon to it. She looks like a child, Flange thought. And the rat like her own child.

And then: I wonder why Cindy and I never had a child.

And: a child makes it all right. Let the world shrink to a *boccie* ball.

So of course he knew.

"Sure," he said. "All right. I'll stay." For a while, at least, he thought. She looked up gravely. Whitecaps danced across her eyes; sea creatures, he knew, would be cruising about in the submarine green of her heart.

ENTROPY

Boris has just given me a summary of his views. He is a
weather prophet. The weather will continue bad, he says.
There will be more calamities, more death, more despair.
Not the slightest indication of a change anywhere. . . .
We must get into step, a lockstep toward the prison of
death. There is no escape. The weather will not change.

— *Tropic of Cancer*

D OWNSTAIRS, Meatball Mulligan's lease-breaking
party was moving into its 40th hour. On the
kitchen floor, amid a litter of empty champagne fifths,
were Sandor Rojas and three friends, playing spit in the
ocean and staying awake on Heidseck and benzedrine
pills. In the living room Duke, Vincent, Krinkles and
Paco sat crouched over a 15-inch speaker which had been
bolted into the top of a wastepaper basket, listening to
27 watts' worth of *The Heroes' Gate at Kiev*. They all
wore hornrimmed sunglasses and rapt expressions, and
smoked funny-looking cigarettes which contained not,
as you might expect, tobacco, but an adulterated form of
cannabis sativa. This group was the Duke di Angelis
quartet. They recorded for a local label called Tambú
and had to their credit one 10″ LP entitled *Songs of
Outer Space*. From time to time one of them would flick
the ashes from his cigarette into the speaker cone to watch
them dance around. Meatball himself was sleeping over
by the window, holding an empty magnum to his chest
as if it were a teddy bear. Several government girls, who

worked for people like the State Department and NSA, had passed out on couches, chairs and in one case the bathroom sink.

This was in early February of '57 and back then there were a lot of American expatriates around Washington, D.C., who would talk, every time they met you, about how someday they were going to go over to Europe for real but right now it seemed they were working for the government. Everyone saw a fine irony in this. They would stage, for instance, polyglot parties where the newcomer was sort of ignored if he couldn't carry on simultaneous conversations in three or four languages. They would haunt Armenian delicatessens for weeks at a stretch and invite you over for bulghour and lamb in tiny kitchens whose walls were covered with bullfight posters. They would have affairs with sultry girls from Andalucía or the Midi who studied economics at Georgetown. Their Dôme was a collegiate Rathskeller out on Wisconsin Avenue called the Old Heidelberg and they had to settle for cherry blossoms instead of lime trees when spring came, but in its lethargic way their life provided, as they said, kicks.

At the moment, Meatball's party seemed to be gathering its second wind. Outside there was rain. Rain splatted against the tar paper on the roof and was fractured into a fine spray off the noses, eyebrows and lips of wooden gargoyles under the eaves, and ran like drool down the windowpanes. The day before, it had snowed and the day before that there had been winds of gale force and before that the sun had made the city glitter bright as April, though the calendar read early February. It is a curious season in Washington, this false spring. Somewhere in it are Lincoln's Birthday and the Chinese New Year, and a forlornness in the streets because cherry blossoms are weeks away still and, as Sarah Vaughan has put it, spring will be a little late this year. Generally crowds like the one which would gather in the Old Heidelberg on weekday afternoons to drink Würtzburger and to sing Lili Marlene (not to mention The Sweetheart of Sigma Chi) are inevitably and incorrigibly Romantic. And as every good Romantic knows, the soul (*spiritus, ruach, pneuma*) is nothing, substantially, but air; it is only natural that warpings in the atmosphere should be recapitulated in those who breathe it. So that over and above the public components – holidays, tourist attractions – there are private meanderings, linked to the climate as if this spell were a *stretto* passage in the year's fugue: haphazard weather, aimless loves, unpredicted commitments: months one can easily spend *in* fugue, because oddly enough, later on, winds, rains, passions of February and March are never remembered in that city, it is as if they had never been.

The last bass notes of *The Heroes' Gate* boomed up through the floor and woke Callisto from an uneasy sleep. The first thing he became aware of was a small bird he had been holding gently between his hands, against his body. He turned his head sidewise on the pillow to smile down at it, at its blue hunched-down head and sick, lidded eyes, wondering how many more nights he would have to give it warmth before it was well again. He had been holding the bird like that for three days: it was the only way he knew to restore its health. Next to him the girl stirred and whimpered, her arm thrown across her face. Mingled with the sounds of the rain came the first tentative, querulous morning voices of the other birds, hidden in philodendrons and small fan palms: patches of scarlet, yellow and blue laced through this Rousseau-like fantasy, this hothouse jungle it had taken him seven years to weave together. Hermetically sealed, it was a tiny enclave of regularity in the city's chaos, alien to the

[*83*]

vagaries of the weather, of national politics, of any civil disorder. Through trial-and-error Callisto had perfected its ecological balance, with the help of the girl its artistic harmony, so that the swayings of its plant life, the stirrings of its birds and human inhabitants were all as integral as the rhythms of a perfectly-executed mobile. He and the girl could no longer, of course, be omitted from that sanctuary; they had become necessary to its unity. What they needed from outside was delivered. They did not go out.

"Is he all right," she whispered. She lay like a tawny question mark facing him, her eyes suddenly huge and dark and blinking slowly. Callisto ran a finger beneath the feathers at the base of the bird's neck; caressed it gently. "He's going to be well, I think. See: he hears his friends beginning to wake up." The girl had heard the rain and the birds even before she was fully awake. Her name was Aubade: she was part French and part Annamese, and she lived on her own curious and lonely planet, where the clouds and the odor of poincianas, the bitterness of wine and the accidental fingers at the small of her back or feathery against her breasts came to her reduced inevitably to the terms of sound: of music which emerged at intervals from a howling darkness of discordancy. "Aubade," he said, "go see." Obedient, she arose; padded to the window, pulled aside the drapes and after a moment said: "It is 37. Still 37." Callisto frowned. "Since Tuesday, then," he said. "No change." Henry Adams, three generations before his own, had stared aghast at Power; Callisto found himself now in much the same state over Thermodynamics, the inner life of that power, realizing like his predecessor that the Virgin and the dynamo stand as much for love as for power; that the two are indeed identical; and that love therefore not only makes the world go round but also

[*84*]

makes the boccie ball spin, the nebula precess. It was this latter or sidereal element which disturbed him. The cosmologists had predicted an eventual heat-death for the universe (something like Limbo: form and motion abolished, heat-energy identical at every point in it); the meteorologists, day-to-day, staved it off by contradicting with a reassuring array of varied temperatures.

But for three days now, despite the changeful weather, the mercury had stayed at 37 degrees Fahrenheit. Leery at omens of apocalypse, Callisto shifted beneath the covers. His fingers pressed the bird more firmly, as if needing some pulsing or suffering assurance of an early break in the temperature.

It was that last cymbal crash that did it. Meatball was hurled wincing into consciousness as the synchronized wagging of heads over the wastebasket stopped. The final hiss remained for an instant in the room, then melted into the whisper of rain outside. "Aarrgghh," announced Meatball in the silence, looking at the empty magnum. Krinkles, in slow motion, turned, smiled and held out a cigarette. "Tea time, man," he said. "No, no," said Meatball. "How many times I got to tell you guys. Not at my place. You ought to know, Washington is lousy with Feds." Krinkles looked wistful. "Jeez, Meatball," he said, "you don't want to do nothing no more." "Hair of dog," said Meatball. "Only hope. Any juice left?" He began to crawl toward the kitchen. "No champagne, I don't think," Duke said. "Case of tequila behind the icebox." They put on an Earl Bostic side. Meatball paused at the kitchen door, glowering at Sandor Rojas. "Lemons," he said after some thought. He crawled to the refrigerator and got out three lemons and some cubes, found the tequila and set about restoring order to his nervous system. He drew blood once cutting the lemons and had to use two hands squeezing them and his foot to crack the ice tray but after about ten minutes he found himself, through some miracle, beaming down into a monster tequila sour. "That looks yummy," Sandor Rojas said. "How about you make me one." Meatball blinked at him. *"Kitchi lofass a shegitbe,"* he replied automatically, and wandered away into the bathroom. "I say," he called out a moment later to no one in particular. "I say, there seems to be a girl or something sleeping in the sink." He took her by the shoulders and shook. "Wha," she said. "You don't look too comfortable," Meatball said. "Well," she agreed. She stumbled to the shower, turned on the cold water and sat down crosslegged in the spray. "That's better," she smiled.

"Meatball," Sandor Rojas yelled from the kitchen. "Somebody is trying to come in the window. A burglar, I think. A second-story man." "What are you worrying about," Meatball said. "We're on the third floor." He loped back into the kitchen. A shaggy woebegone figure stood out on the fire escape, raking his fingernails down the windowpane. Meatball opened the window. "Saul," he said.

"Sort of wet out," Saul said. He climbed in, dripping. "You heard, I guess."

"Miriam left you," Meatball said, "or something, is all I heard."

There was a sudden flurry of knocking at the front door. "Do come in," Sandor Rojas called. The door opened and there were three coeds from George Washington, all of whom were majoring in philosophy. They were each holding a gallon of Chianti. Sandor leaped up and dashed into the living room. "We heard there was a party," one blonde said. "Young blood," Sandor shouted. He was an ex-Hungarian freedom fighter who had easily the worst chronic case of what certain critics of the middle class have called Don Giovannism in the District of Columbia.

Purche porti la gonnella, voi sapete quel che fa. Like Pavlov's dog: a contralto voice or a whiff of Arpège and Sandor would begin to salivate. Meatball regarded the trio blearily as they filed into the kitchen; he shrugged. "Put the wine in the icebox," he said "and good morning."

Aubade's neck made a golden bow as she bent over the sheets of foolscap, scribbling away in the green murk of the room. "As a young man at Princeton," Callisto was dictating, nestling the bird against the gray hairs of his chest, "Callisto had learned a mnemonic device for remembering the Laws of Thermodynamics: you can't win, things are going to get worse before they get better, who says they're going to get better. At the age of 54, confronted with Gibbs' notion of the universe, he suddenly realized that undergraduate cant had been oracle, after all. That spindly maze of equations became, for him, a vision of ultimate, cosmic heat-death. He had known all along, of course, that nothing but a theoretical engine or system ever runs at 100% efficiency; and about the theorem of Clausius, which states that the entropy of an isolated system always continually increases. It was not, however, until Gibbs and Boltzmann brought to this principle the methods of statistical mechanics that the horrible significance of it all dawned on him: only then did he realize that the isolated system – galaxy, engine, human being, culture, whatever – must evolve spontaneously toward the Condition of the More Probable. He was forced, therefore, in the sad dying fall of middle age, to a radical reëvaluation of everything he had learned up to then; all the cities and seasons and casual passions of his days had now to be looked at in a new and elusive light. He did not know if he was equal to the task. He was aware of the dangers of the reductive fallacy and, he hoped, strong enough not to drift into the graceful decadence of an enervated fatalism. His had always been a vigorous, Italian sort of pessimism: like Machiavelli, he allowed the forces of *virtù* and *fortuna* to be about 50/50; but the equations now introduced a random factor which pushed the odds to some unutterable and indeterminate ratio which he found himself afraid to calculate." Around him loomed vague hothouse shapes; the pitifully small heart fluttered against his own. Counter-pointed against his words the girl heard the chatter of birds and fitful car honkings scattered along the wet morning and Earl Bostic's alto rising in occasional wild peaks through the floor. The architectonic purity of her world was constantly threatened by such hints of anarchy: gaps and excrescences and skew lines, and a shifting or tilting of planes to which she had continually to readjust lest the whole structure shiver into a disarray of discrete and meaningless signals. Callisto had described the process once as a kind of "feedback": she crawled into dreams each night with a sense of exhaustion, and a desperate resolve never to relax that vigilance. Even in the brief periods when Callisto made love to her, soaring above the bowing of taut nerves in haphazard double-stops would be the one singing string of her determination.

"Nevertheless," continued Callisto, "he found in entropy or the measure of disorganization for a closed system an adequate metaphor to apply to certain phenomena in his own world. He saw, for example, the younger generation responding to Madison Avenue with the same spleen his own had once reserved for Wall Street: and in American 'consumerism' discovered a similar tendency from the least to the most probable, from differentiation to sameness, from ordered individuality to a kind of chaos. He found himself, in short, restating Gibbs' prediction in social terms, and envisioned a heat-death for his culture in which ideas, like heat-energy, would no longer be transferred, since each point in it would ultimately have the same quantity of energy; and intellectual motion would, accordingly, cease." He glanced up suddenly. "Check it now," he said. Again she rose and peered out at the thermometer. "37," she said. "The rain has stopped." He bent his head quickly and held his lips against a quivering wing. "Then it will change soon," he said, trying to keep his voice firm.

Sitting on the stove Saul was like any big rag doll that a kid has been taking out some incomprehensible rage on. "What happened," Meatball said. "If you feel like talking, I mean."

"Of course I feel like talking," Saul said. "One thing I did, I slugged her."

"Discipline must be maintained."

"Ha, ha. I wish you'd been there. Oh Meatball, it was a lovely fight. She ended up throwing a *Handbook of Chemistry and Physics* at me, only it missed and went through the window, and when the glass broke I reckon something in her broke too. She stormed out of the house crying, out in the rain. No raincoat or anything."

"She'll be back."

"No."

"Well." Soon Meatball said: "It was something earth-shattering, no doubt. Like who is better, Sal Mineo or Ricky Nelson."

"What it was about," Saul said, "was communication theory. Which of course makes it very hilarious."

"I don't know anything about communication theory."

"Neither does my wife. Come right down to it, who does? That's the joke."

When Meatball saw the kind of smile Saul had on his face he said: "Maybe you would like tequila or something."

"No. I mean, I'm sorry. It's a field you can go off the deep end in, is all. You get where you're watching all the time for security cops: behind bushes, around corners. MUFFET is top secret."

"Wha."

"Multi-unit factorial field electronic tabulator."

"You were fighting about that."

"Miriam has been reading science fiction again. That and *Scientific American*. It seems she is, as we say, bugged at this idea of computers acting like people. I made the mistake of saying you can just as well turn that around, and talk about human behavior like a program fed into an IBM machine."

"Why not," Meatball said.

"Indeed, why not. In fact it is sort of crucial to communication, not to mention information theory. Only when I said that she hit the roof. Up went the balloon. And I can't figure out *why*. If anybody should know why, I should. I refuse to believe the government is wasting taxpayers' money on me, when it has so many bigger and better things to waste it on."

Meatball made a moue. "Maybe she thought you were acting like a cold, dehumanized amoral scientist type."

"My god," Saul flung up an arm. "Dehumanized. How much more human can I get? I worry, Meatball, I do. There are Europeans wandering around North Africa these days with their tongues torn out of their heads because those tongues have spoken the wrong words. Only the Europeans thought they were the right words."

"Language barrier," Meatball suggested.

Saul jumped down off the stove. "That," he said, angry, "is a good candidate for sick joke of the year. No, ace, it is *not* a barrier. If it is anything it's a kind of leakage. Tell a girl: 'I love you.' No trouble with two-thirds of that, it's a closed circuit. Just you and she. But that nasty four-letter word in the middle, *that's* the one you have to look out for. Ambiguity. Redundance. Irrelevance, even. Leakage. All this is noise. Noise screws up your signal, makes for disorganization in the circuit."

Meatball shuffled around. "Well, now, Saul," he muttered, "you're sort of, I don't know, expecting a lot from people. I mean, you know. What it is is, most of the things we say, I guess, are mostly noise."

"Ha! Half of what you just said, for example."

"Well, you do it too."

"I know." Saul smiled grimly. "It's a bitch, ain't it."

"I bet that's what keeps divorce lawyers in business. Whoops."

"Oh I'm not sensitive. Besides," frowning, "you're right. You find I think that most 'successful' marriages – Miriam and me, up to last night – are sort of founded on compromises. You never run at top efficiency, usually all you have is a minimum basis for a workable thing. I believe the phrase is Togetherness."

"Aarrgghh."

"Exactly. You find that one a bit noisy, don't you. But the noise content is different for each of us because you're a bachelor and I'm not. Or wasn't. The hell with it."

"Well sure," Meatball said, trying to be helpful, "you were using different words. By 'human being' you meant something that you can look at like it was a computer. It helps you think better on the job or something. But Miriam meant something entirely – "

"The hell with it."

Meatball fell silent. "I'll take that drink," Saul said after a while.

The card game had been abandoned and Sandor's friends were slowly getting wasted on tequila. On the living room couch, one of the coeds and Krinkles were engaged in amorous conversation. "No," Krinkles was saying, "no, I can't put Dave *down*. In fact I give Dave a lot of credit, man. Especially considering his accident and all." The girl's smile faded. "How terrible," she said. "What accident?" "Hadn't you heard?" Krinkles said. "When Dave was in the army, just a private E-2, they sent him down to Oak Ridge on special duty. Something to do with the Manhattan Project. He was handling hot stuff one day and got an overdose of radiation. So now he's got to wear lead gloves all the time." She shook her head sympathetically. "What an awful break for a piano-player."

Meatball had abandoned Saul to a bottle of tequila and was about to go to sleep in a closet when the front door flew open and the place was invaded by five enlisted personnel of the U.S. Navy, all in varying stages of abomination. "This is the place," shouted a fat, pimply seaman apprentice who had lost his white hat. "This here is the hoorhouse that chief was telling us about." A stringy-looking 3rd class boatswain's mate pushed him aside and cased the living room. "You're right, Slab," he said. "But it don't look like much, even for Stateside. I seen better tail in Naples, Italy." "How much, hey," boomed a large seaman with adenoids, who was holding a Mason jar full of white lightning. "Oh, my god," said Meatball.

Outside the temperature remained constant at 37 degrees Fahrenheit. In the hothouse Aubade stood absently caressing the branches of a young mimosa, hearing a motif of sap-rising, the rough and unresolved anticipatory theme of those fragile pink blossoms which, it is said, insure fertility. That music rose in a tangled tracery: arabesques of order competing fugally with the improvised discords of the party downstairs, which peaked sometimes in cusps and ogees of noise. That precious signal-to-noise ratio, whose delicate balance required every calorie of her strength, seesawed inside the small tenuous skull as she watched Callisto, sheltering the bird. Callisto was trying to confront any idea of the heat-death now, as he nuzzled the feathery lump in his hands. He sought correspondences. Sade, of course. And Temple Drake, gaunt and hopeless in her little park in Paris, at the end of *Sanctuary*. Final equilibrium. *Nightwood*. And the tango. Any tango, but more than any perhaps the sad sick dance in Stravinsky's *L'Histoire du Soldat*. He thought back: what had tango music been for them after the war, what meanings had he missed in all the stately coupled automatons in the *cafés-dansants,* or in the metronomes which had ticked behind the eyes of his own partners? Not even the clean constant winds of Switzerland could cure the *grippe espagnole*: Stravinsky had had it, they all had had it. And how many musicians were left after Passchendaele, after the Marne? It came down in this case to seven: violin, double-bass. Clarinet, bassoon. Cornet, trombone. Tympani. Almost as if any tiny troupe of saltimbanques had set about conveying the same information as a full pit-orchestra. There was hardly a full complement left in Europe. Yet with violin and tympani Stravinsky had managed to communicate in that tango the same exhaustion, the same airlessness one saw in the slicked-down youths who were trying to imitate Vernon Castle, and in their mistresses, who simply did not care. *Ma maîtresse.* Celeste. Returning to Nice after the second war he had found that café replaced by a perfume shop which catered to American tourists. And no secret vestige of her in the cobblestones or in the old pension next door; no perfume to match her breath heavy with the sweet Spanish wine she always drank. And so instead he had purchased a Henry Miller novel and left for Paris, and read the book on the train so that when he arrived he had been given at least a little forewarning. And saw that Celeste and the others and even Temple Drake were not all that had changed. "Aubade," he said, "my head aches." The sound of his voice generated in the girl an answering scrap of melody. Her movement toward the kitchen, the towel, the cold water, and his eyes following her formed a weird and intricate canon; as she placed the compress on his forehead his sigh of gratitude seemed to signal a new subject, another series of modulations.

"No," Meatball was still saying, "no, I'm afraid not. This is not a house of ill repute. I'm sorry, really I am." Slab was adamant. "But the chief said," he kept repeating. The seaman offered to swap the moonshine for a good piece. Meatball looked around frantically, as if seeking assistance. In the middle of the room, the Duke di Angelis quartet were engaged in a historic moment. Vincent was seated and the others standing: they were going through the motions of a group having a session, only without instruments. "I say," Meatball said. Duke moved his head a few times, smiled faintly, lit a cigarette, and eventually caught sight of Meatball. "Quiet, man," he whispered. Vincent began to fling his arms around, his fists clenched; then, abruptly, was still, then repeated the performance. This went on for a few minutes while Meatball sipped his drink moodily. The navy had withdrawn to the kitchen. Finally at some invisible signal the group stopped tapping their feet and Duke grinned and said, "At least we ended together."

Meatball glared at him. "I say," he said. "I have this new conception, man," Duke said. "You remember your namesake. You remember Gerry."

"No," said Meatball. "I'll remember April, if that's any help."

"As a matter of fact," Duke said, "it was Love for Sale. Which shows how much you know. The point is, it was Mulligan, Chet Baker and that crew, way back then, out yonder. You dig?"

"Baritone sax," Meatball said. "Something about a baritone sax."

"But no piano, man. No guitar. Or accordion. You know what that means."

"Not exactly," Meatball said.

"Well first let me just say, that I am no Mingus, no John Lewis. Theory was never my strong point. I mean things like reading were always difficult for me and all – "

"I know," Meatball said drily. "You got your card taken away because you changed key on Happy Birthday at a Kiwanis Club picnic."

"Rotarian. But it occurred to me, in one of these flashes of insight, that if that first quartet of Mulligan's had no piano, it could only mean one thing."

"No chords," said Paco, the baby-faced bass.

"What he is trying to say," Duke said, "is no root chords. Nothing to listen to while you blow a horizontal line. What one does in such a case is, one *thinks* the roots."

A horrified awareness was dawning on Meatball. "And the next logical extension," he said.

"Is to think everything," Duke announced with simple dignity. "Roots, line, everything."

Meatball looked at Duke, awed. "But," he said.

"Well," Duke said modestly, "there are a few bugs to work out."

"But," Meatball said.

"Just listen," Duke said. "You'll catch on." And off they went again into orbit, presumably somewhere around the asteroid belt. After a while Krinkles made an embouchure and started moving his fingers and Duke clapped his hand to his forehead. "Oaf!" he roared. "The new head we're using, you remember, I wrote last night?" "Sure," Krinkles said, "the new head. I come in on the bridge. All your heads I come in then." "Right," Duke said. "So why – " "Wha," said Krinkles, "16 bars, I wait, I come in – " "16?" Duke said. "No. No, Krinkles. Eight you waited. You want me to sing it? A cigarette that bears a lipstick's traces, an airline ticket to romantic places." Krinkles scratched his head. "These Foolish Things, you mean." "Yes," Duke said, "yes, Krinkles. Bravo." "Not I'll Remember April," Krinkles said. "*Minghe morte,*" said Duke. "I *figured* we were playing it a little slow," Krinkles said. Meatball chuckled. "Back to the old drawing board," he said. "No, man," Duke said, "back to the airless void." And they took off again, only it seemed Paco was playing in G sharp while the rest were in E flat, so they had to start all over.

In the kitchen two of the girls from George Washington and the sailors were singing Let's All Go Down and Piss on the Forrestal. There was a two-handed, bilingual *morra* game on over by the icebox. Saul had filled several paper bags with water and was sitting on the fire escape, dropping them on passersby in the street. A fat government girl in a Bennington sweatshirt, recently engaged to an ensign attached to the Forrestal, came charging into the kitchen, head lowered, and butted Slab in the stomach. Figuring this was as good an excuse for a fight as any, Slab's buddies piled in. The *morra* players were nose-to-nose, screaming *trois, sette* at the tops of their lungs. From the shower the girl Meatball had taken out of the sink announced that she was drowning. She had apparently sat on the drain and the water was now up to her neck. The noise in Meatball's apartment had reached a sustained, ungodly crescendo.

Meatball stood and watched, scratching his stomach lazily. The way he figured, there were only about two ways he could cope: (a) lock himself in the closet and maybe eventually they would all go away, or (b) try to calm everybody down, one by one. (a) was certainly the more attractive alternative. But then he started thinking about that closet. It was dark and stuffy and he would be alone. He did not feature being alone. And then this crew off the good ship Lollipop or whatever it was might take it upon themselves to kick down the closet door, for a lark. And if that happened he would be, at the very least, embarrassed. The other way was more a pain in the neck, but probably better in the long run.

So he decided to try and keep his lease-breaking party from deteriorating into total chaos: he gave wine to the sailors and separated the *morra* players; he introduced the fat government girl to Sandor Rojas, who would keep her out of trouble; he helped the girl in the shower to dry off and get into bed; he had another talk with Saul; he called a repairman for the refrigerator, which someone had discovered was on the blink. This is what he did until nightfall, when most of the revellers had passed out and the party trembled on the threshold of its third day.

Upstairs Callisto, helpless in the past, did not feel the faint rhythm inside the bird begin to slacken and fail. Aubade was by the window, wandering the ashes of her own lovely world; the temperature held steady, the sky had become a uniform darkening gray. Then something from downstairs — a girl's scream, an overturned chair, a glass dropped on the floor, he would never know what exactly — pierced that private time-warp and he became aware of the faltering, the constriction of muscles, the tiny tossings of the bird's head; and his own pulse began to pound more fiercely, as if trying to compensate. "Aubade," he called weakly, "he's dying." The girl, flowing and rapt, crossed the hothouse to gaze down at Callisto's hands. The two remained like that, poised, for one minute, and two, while the heartbeat ticked a graceful diminuendo down at last into stillness. Callisto raised his head slowly. "I held him," he protested, impotent with the wonder of it, "to give him the warmth of my body. Almost as if I were communicating life to him, or a sense of life. What has happened? Has the transfer of heat ceased to work? Is there no more . . ." He did not finish.

"I was just at the window," she said. He sank back, terrified. She stood a moment more, irresolute; she had sensed his obsession long ago, realized somehow that that constant 37 was now decisive. Suddenly then, as if seeing the single and unavoidable conclusion to all this she moved swiftly to the window before Callisto could speak; tore away the drapes and smashed out the glass with two exquisite hands which came away bleeding and glistening with splinters; and turned to face the man on the bed and wait with him until the moment of equilibrium was reached, when 37 degrees Fahrenheit should prevail both outside and inside, and forever, and the hovering, curious dominant of their separate lives should resolve into a tonic of darkness and the final absence of all motion.

UNDER THE ROSE

As the afternoon progressed, yellow clouds began to gather over Place Mohammed Ali, casting a tendril or two back toward the Libyan desert. A wind from the southwest swept quietly up rue Ibrahim and across the square, bringing the chill of the desert into the city.

Then let it rain, Porpentine thought: rain soon. He sat at a small wrought-iron table in front of a café, smoking Turkish cigarettes with a third cup of coffee, ulster thrown over the back of an adjoining chair. Today he wore light tweeds and a felt hat with muslin tied round it to protect his neck from the sun; he was leery of the sun. Clouds moved in now to dim it out. Porpentine shifted in his seat, took a watch from his waistcoat pocket, consulted it, replaced it. Turned once more to look out at the Europeans milling about the square: some hurrying into the Banque Impériale Ottomane, others lingering by shopwindows, seating themselves at cafés. His face was carefully arranged: nerveless, rakish-expectant; he might have been there to meet a lady.

All for the benefit of anyone who cared. God knew how many there were. In practice it narrowed down to those in the employ of Moldweorp, the veteran spy. One somehow always tacked on "the veteran spy." It might have been a throwback to an earlier time, when such epithets were one reward for any proof of heroism or manhood. Or possibly because now, with a century rushing headlong to its end and with it a tradition in espionage where everything was tacitly on a gentlemanly basis, where the playing-fields of Eton had conditioned (one might say) premilitary conduct as well, the label was a way of fixing identity in this special *haut monde* before death – individual or collective – stung it to stillness forever. Porpentine himself was called *"il semplice inglese"* by those who cared.

Last week in Brindisi their compassion had been relentless as always; it gave them a certain moral advantage, realizing as they did that Porpentine was somehow incapable of returning it. Tender and sheepish, therefore, they wove their paths to cross his own at random. Mirrored, too, his private tactics: living in the most frequented hotels, sitting at the tourist cafés, traveling always by the respectable, public routes. Which surely upset him most; as if, Porpentine once having fashioned such proper innocence, any use of it by others – especially Moldweorp's agents – involved some violation of patent right. They would pirate if they could his child's gaze, his plump angel's smile. For nearly fifteen years he'd fled their sympathy; since the lobby of the Hotel Bristol, Naples, on a winter evening in '83, when everyone you knew in spying's freemasonry seemed to be waiting. For Khartum to fall, for the crisis in Afghanistan to keep growing until it could be given the name of sure apocalypse. There he had come, as he'd known he must at some stage of the game, to face the already aged face of Moldweorp himself,

the prizeman or maestro, feel the old man's hand solicitous on his arm and hear the earnest whisper: "Things
are reaching a head; we may be for it, all of us. Do be
careful." What response? What possible? Only a scrutiny,
almost desperate, for any fine trace of insincerity. Of
course he'd found none there; and so turned, quickly,
flaming, unable to cover a certain helplessness. Hoist thus
by his own petard at every subsequent encounter as well,
Porpentine by the dog-days of '98 seemed, in contrast,
to have grown cold, unkind. They would continue to use
so fortunate an engine: would never seek his life, violate
The Rules, forbear what had become for them pleasure.

He sat now wondering if either of the two at Brindisi
had followed him to Alexandria. Certain he had seen
no one on the Venice boat, he reviewed possibilities.
An Austrian Lloyd steamer from Trieste also touched
at Brindisi; was the only other they would have taken.
Today was Monday. Porpentine had left on a Friday.
The Trieste boat left on Thursday and arrived late Sunday.
So that (a) at second-worst he had six days, or (b) at
worst, they knew. In which case they had left the day
before Porpentine and were already here.

He watched the sun darken and the wind flutter the
leaves of acacias around Place Mohammed Ali. In the
distance his name was being called. He turned to watch
Goodfellow, blond and jovial, striding toward him down
rue Cherif Pacha, wearing a dress suit and a pith helmet
two sizes too large. "I say," Goodfellow cried. "Porpentine,
I've met a remarkable young lady." Porpentine lit another
cigarette and closed his eyes. All of Goodfellow's young
ladies were remarkable. After two and a half years as
partners one got used to an incidental progress of feminine
attachments to Goodfellow's right arm: as if every capital
of Europe were Margate and the promenade a continent
long. If Goodfellow knew half his salary was sent out

[*103*]

every month to a wife in Liverpool he showed none of it, rollicking along unperturbed, cock-a-hoop. Porpentine had seen his running mate's dossier but decided some time ago that the wife at least was none of his affair. He listened now as Goodfellow drew up a chair and summoned a waiter in wretched Arabic: *"Hat fingan kahwa bisukkar, ya weled."*

"Goodfellow," Porpentine said, "you don't have to –"

"Ya weled, ya weled," Goodfellow roared. The waiter was French and did not understand Arabic. "Ah," Goodfellow said, "coffee then. *Café,* you know."

"How are the digs?" asked Porpentine.

"First-rate." Goodfellow was staying at the Hotel Khedival, seven blocks away. There being a temporary hitch in finances, only one could afford the usual accommodations. Porpentine was staying with a friend in the Turkish quarter. "About this girl," Goodfellow said. "Party tonight at the Austrian Consulate. Her escort, Goodfellow: linguist, adventurer, diplomat . . ."

"Name," said Porpentine.

"Victoria Wren. Traveling with family, *videlicet:* Sir Alastair Wren, F.R.C.O., sister Mildred. Mother deceased. Departing for Cairo tomorrow. Cook's tour down the Nile." Porpentine waited. "Lunatic archaeologist," Goodfellow seemed reluctant. "One Bongo-Shaftsbury. Young, addlepated. Harmless."

"Aha."

"Tch-tch. Too highly strung. Should drink less café-fort."

"Possibly," Porpentine said. Goodfellow's coffee arrived. Porpentine continued: "You know we'll end up chancing it anyway. We always do." Goodfellow grinned absently and stirred his coffee.

"I have already taken steps. Bitter rivalry for the young lady's attentions between myself and Bongo-Shaftsbury.

Fellow is a perfect ass. Is mad to see the Theban ruins at Luxor."

"Of course," Porpentine said. He arose and tossed the ulster around his shoulders. It had begun to rain. Goodfellow handed him a small white envelope with the Austrian crest on the back.

"Eight, I suppose," said Porpentine.

"Right you are. You must see this girl."

It was then that one of Porpentine's seizures came upon him. The profession was lonely and in constant though not always deadly earnest. At regular intervals he found need to play the buffoon. "A bit of skylarking," he called it. It made him, he believed, more human. "I will be there with false mustaches," he now informed Goodfellow, "impersonating an Italian count." He stood gaily at attention, pressed an imaginary hand: *Carissima signorina.*" He bowed, kissed the air.

"You're insane," from Goodfellow, amiable.

"Pazzo son!" Porpentine began to sing in a wavering tenor. *"Guardate, come io piango ed imploro . . ."* His Italian was not perfect. Cockney inflections danced through. A group of English tourists, hurrying in out of the rain, glanced back at him, curious.

"Enough," Goodfellow winced. "'Twas Turin, I remember. Torino. Was it not? '93. I escorted a marchesina with a mole on her back and Cremonini sang Des Grieux. You, Porpentine, desecrate the memory."

But the antic Porpentine leaped in the air, clicked his heels; stood posturing, fist on chest, the other arm outstretched. *"Come io chiedo pietà!"* The waiter looked on with a pained smile; it began to rain harder. Goodfellow sat in the rain sipping his coffee. Drops of rain rattled on the pith helmet. "The sister isn't bad," he observed as Porpentine frolicked out in the square. "Mildred, you know. Though only eleven." At length it occurred to him that his dress suit was becoming soaked. He arose, left a piastre and a millième on the table and nodded to Porpentine, who now stood watching him. The square was empty except for the equestrian statue of Mohammed Ali. How many times had they faced each other this way, dwarfed horizontal and vertical by any plaza's late-afternoon landscape? Could an argument from design be predicated on that moment only, then the two must have been displaceable, like minor chess-pieces, anywhere across the board of Europe. Both of a color (though one hanging back diagonal in deference to his chief), both scanning any embassy's parquetry for signs of the Opposition, any statue's face for a reassurance of self-agency (perhaps, unhappily, self-humanity), they would try not to remember that every city's square, however you cut it, remains inanimate after all. Soon the two men turned almost formally, to part in opposite directions: Goodfellow back toward the hotel, Porpentine into rue Ras-et-Tin and the Turkish quarter. Until 8:00 he would ponder the Situation.

At the moment it was a bad job all round. Sirdar Kitchener, England's newest colonial hero, recently victorious at Khartum, was just now some four hundred miles farther down the White Nile, foraging about in the jungle. A General Marchand was also rumored to be in the vicinity. Britain wanted no part of France in the Nile Valley. M. Delcassé, Foreign Minister of a newly formed French cabinet, would as soon go to war as not if there were any trouble when the two detachments met. As meet, everyone realized by now, they would. Kitchener had been instructed not to take any offensive and to avoid all provocation. Russia would support France in case of war, while England had a temporary rapprochement with Germany, which of course meant Italy and Austria as well.

Moldweorp's chief amusement, Porpentine reflected,

had always been to harass. All he asked was that eventually there be a war. Not just a small incidental skirmish in the race to carve up Africa, but one pip-pip, jolly-ho, up-goes-the-balloon Armageddon for Europe. Once Porpentine might have been puzzled that his opposite number should desire war so passionately. Now he took it for granted that at some point in these fifteen years of hare-and-hounds he himself had conceived the private mission of keeping off Armageddon. An alignment like this, he felt, could only have taken place in a Western World where spying was becoming less an individual than a group enterprise, where the events of 1848 and the activities of anarchists and radicals all over the Continent seemed to proclaim that history was being made no longer through the *virtù* of single princes but rather by man in the mass; by trends and tendencies and impersonal curves on a lattice of pale blue lines. So it was inevitably single combat between the veteran spy and *il semplice inglese*. They stood alone – God knew where – on deserted lists. Goodfellow knew of the private battle, as doubtless did Moldweorp's subordinates. They all took on the roles of solicitous seconds, attending to the strictly national interests while their chiefs circled and parried above them on some unreachable level. It happened that Porpentine worked nominally for England and Moldweorp for Germany, but this was accident: they would probably have chosen the same sides had their employments been reversed. For he and Moldweorp, Porpentine knew, were cut from the same pattern: comrade Machiavellians, still playing the games of Renaissance Italian politics in a world that had outgrown them. The self-assumed roles became only, then, assertions of a kind of pride, first of all in a profession which still remembered the freebooting agility of Lord Palmerston. Fortunately for Porpentine the Foreign Office had enough of the old spirit left to

[*107*]

give him nearly a free hand. Although if they did suspect he'd have no way of knowing. Where his personal mission coincided with diplomatic policy, Porpentine would send back a report to London, and no one ever seemed to complain.

The key man now for Porpentine seemed to be Lord Cromer, the British Consul-General at Cairo, an extremely able diplomat and cautious enough to avoid any rash impulses: war, for example. Could Moldweorp have an assassination in the works? A trip to Cairo seemed in order. As innocent as possible; that went without saying.

The Austrian Consulate was across the street from the Hotel Khedival, the festivities there unexceptional. Goodfellow sat at the bottom of a wide flight of marble steps with a girl who could not have been more than eighteen and who, like the gown she wore, seemed awkwardly bouffant and provincial. The rain had shrunken Goodfellow's formal attire; his coat looked tight under the armpits and across the stomach; the blond hair had been disarranged by the desert wind, the face was flushed, uncomfortable. Watching him, Porpentine came aware of his own appearance: quaint, anomalous, his evening clothes purchased the same year General Gordon was done in by the Mahdi. Hopelessly passé at gatherings like this, he often played a game in which he was, say, Gordon returned from the dead and headless; that odd, at least, among a resplendent muster of stars, ribbons, and exotic Orders. That out of date, certainly: the Sirdar had retaken Khartum, the outrage was avenged, but people had forgotten. He'd seen the fabled hero of the China wars once, standing on the ramparts at Gravesend. At the time Porpentine had been ten or so and likely to be dazzled; he was. But something had happened between there and the Hotel Bristol. He had thought about

[*108*]

Moldweorp that night and about the likelihood of some apocalypse; perhaps a little too on his own sense of estrangement. But not at all about Chinese Gordon, lonely and enigmatic at the mouth of that boyhood Thames; whose hair it was said had turned white in the space of a day as he waited for death in the besieged city of Khartum.

Porpentine looked about the Consulate, checking off diplomatic personnel: Sir Charles Cookson, Mr. Hewat, M. Girard, Hr. von Hartmann, Cav. Romano, Comte de Zogheb, &c., &c. Right ho. All present and accounted for. Except for the Russian Vice-Consul, M. de Villiers. And oddly enough one's host, Count Khevenhüller-Metsch. Could they be together?

He moved over to the steps where Goodfellow sat desperate, yarning about nonexistent adventures in South Africa. The girl regarded him breathless and smiling. Porpentine wondered if he should sing: It isn't the girl I saw you with in Brighton; who, who, who's your lady friend? He said:

"I say." Goodfellow, relieved and more enthusiastic than necessary, introduced them.

"Miss Victoria Wren."

Porpentine smiled, nodded, searched all over for a cigarette. "How do you do, Miss."

"She's been hearing about our show with Dr. Jameson and the Boers," said Goodfellow.

"You were in the Transvaal together," the girl marveled. Porpentine thought: he can do whatever he wants with this one. Whatever he asks her.

"We've been together for some time, Miss." She bloomed, she billowed; Porpentine, shy, withdrew behind pale cheeks, pursed lips. As if her glow were a reminder of any Yorkshire sunset, or at least some vestige of a vision of Home which neither he nor Goodfellow could afford –

or when you came down to it, cared – to remember, they did share in her presence this common evasiveness.

A low growl sounded behind Porpentine. Goodfellow cringed, smiled weakly, introduced Sir Alastair Wren, Victoria's father. It became clear almost immediately that he was not fond of Goodfellow. With him was a robust, myopic girl of eleven; the sister. Mildred was in Egypt, she soon informed Porpentine, to gather rock specimens, being daft for rocks in the same way Sir Alastair was for large and ancient pipe-organs. He had toured Germany the previous year, alienating the populations of various cathedral towns by recruiting small boys to toil away half-days at a clip keeping the bellows going: and then underpaying. Frightfully, added Victoria. There was, he continued, no decent pipe-organ anywhere on the African continent (which Porpentine could hardly doubt). Goodfellow mentioned an enthusiasm for the barrel-organ, and had Sir Alastair ever tried his hand at one. The peer growled ominously. Out of the corner of his eye Porpentine saw Count Khevenhüller-Metsch come out of an adjoining room, steering the Russian Vice-Consul by the arm and talking wistfully; M. de Villiers punctuated the conversation with mirthful little barks. Aha, Porpentine thought. Mildred had produced from her reticule a large rock, which she now held up to Porpentine for inspection. She had found it out near the site of the ancient Pharos, it contained trilobite fossils. Porpentine could not respond; it was his old weakness. A bar was set up on the mezzanine; he loped up the marble stairs after promising to bring punch (lemonade, of course, for Mildred).

Someone touched his arm as he waited at the bar. He turned and saw one of the two from Brindisi, who said: "Lovely girl." It was the first word he could remember any of them speaking to him directly in fifteen years. He only wondered, uneasy, if they reserved such artifice for times of singular crisis. He picked up the drinks, smiled all angelic; turned, started down the stairs. On the second step he tripped and fell: proceeded whirling and bouncing, followed by sounds of glass breaking and a spray of Chablis punch and lemonade, to the bottom. He'd learned in the army how to take falls. He looked up bashful at Sir Alastair Wren, who nodded in approval.

"Saw a fellow do that in a music-hall once," he said. "You're much better, Porpentine. Really."

"Do it again," Mildred said. Porpentine extracted a cigarette, lay there for a bit smoking. "How about late supper at the Fink," Goodfellow suggested. Porpentine got to his feet. "You remember the chaps we met in Brindisi." Goodfellow nodded, impassive, betraying no tics or tightenings; one of the things Porpentine admired him for. But: "Going home," Sir Alastair muttered, yanking fiercely at Mildred's hand. "Behave yourselves." So Porpentine found himself playing chaperon. He proposed another try for punch. When they got to the mezzanine Moldweorp's man had disappeared. Porpentine wedged one foot between the balusters and looked down, surveying rapidly the faces below. "No," he said. Goodfellow handed him a cup of punch.

"I can't wait to see the Nile," Victoria had been saying, "the pyramids, the Sphinx."

"Cairo," Goodfellow added.

"Yes," Porpentine agreed, "Cairo."

Directly across rue de Rosette was the Fink restaurant. They dashed across the street through the rain, Victoria's cloak ballooning about her; she laughed, delighted with the rain. The crowd inside was entirely European. Porpentine recognized a few faces from the Venice boat. After her first glass of white Vöslauer the girl began to talk. Blithe and so green, she pronounced her *o*'s with a sigh, as if fainting from love. She was Catholic; had been to a convent school near her home, a place called Lardwick-in-the-Fen. This was her first trip abroad. She talked a great deal about her religion: had, for a time, considered the son of God as a young lady will consider any eligible bachelor. But had realized eventually that of course he was not but maintained instead an immense harem clad in black, decked with rosaries. She would never stand for such competition, had therefore left the novitiate after a matter of weeks but not the Church: that, with its sad-faced statuary, its odor of candles and incense, formed along with an uncle Evelyn the twin foci of her serene orbit. The uncle, a wild or renegade sundowner, would arrive from Australia once a year bringing no gifts but prepared to weave as many yarns as the sisters could cope with. As far as Victoria remembered, he had never repeated himself. So she was given enough material to evolve between visits a private and imaginary sphere of influence, which she played with and within constantly: developing, exploring, manipulating. Especially during Mass: for here was the stage, the dramatic field already prepared, serviceable to a seedtime fancy. And so it came about that God wore a wide-awake hat and fought skirmishes with an aboriginal Satan out at the antipodes of the firmament, in the name and for the safekeeping of any Victoria.

Now the desire to feel pity can be seductive; it was always so for Porpentine. At this point he could only flick a rapid glance at Goodfellow's face and think with the sort of admiration pity once foundered in makes detestable: a stroke of genius, the Jameson raid. He chose that, he knew. He always knows. So do I.

One had to. He'd realized long before that women had no monopoly on what is called intuition; that in most men the faculty was latent, only becoming developed or painfully heightened at all in professions like this. But men being positivists and women more dreamy, having hunches still remained at base a feminine talent; so that like it or not they all – Moldweorp, Goodfellow, the pair from Brindisi – had to be part woman. Perhaps even in this maintenance of a threshold for compassion one dared not go beneath was some sort of recognition.

But like a Yorkshire sunset, certain things could not be afforded. Porpentine had realized this as a fledgling. You do not feel pity for the men you have to kill or the people you have to hurt. You do not feel any more than a vague *esprit de corps* toward the agents you are working with. Above all, you do not fall in love. Not if you want to succeed in espionage. God knew what pre-adolescent agonies were responsible; but somehow Porpentine had remained true to that code. He had grown up possessing a sly mind and was too honest not to use it. He stole from street-hawkers, could stack a deck at fifteen, would run away whenever fighting was useless. So that at some point, prowling any mews or alley in midcentury London, the supreme rightness of "the game for its own sake" must have occurred to him, and acted as an irresistible vector aimed toward 1900. Now he would say that any itinerary, with all its doublings-back, emergency stops, and hundred-kilometer feints remained transitory or accidental. Certainly it was convenient, necessary; but never gave an indication of the deeper truth that all of them operated in no conceivable Europe but rather in a zone forsaken by God, between the tropics of diplomacy, lines they were forbidden forever to cross. One had con-sequently to play that idealized colonial Englishman who, alone in the jungle, shaves every day, dresses for dinner every night, and is committed to St. George and no quarter as an article of love. Curious irony in that, of course. Porpentine grimaced to himself. Because both sides, his and Moldweorp's, had each in a different way done the unforgivable: had gone native. Somehow it had come about that one day neither man cared any longer which government he was working for. As if that prospect of a Final Clash were unable by men like them, through whatever frenzied twists and turns, to be evaded. Something had come to pass: who could guess what, or even when? In the Crimea, at Spicheren, at Khartum; it could make no difference. But so suddenly that there was a finite leap or omission in the maturing process – one fell asleep exhausted among immediacies: F.O. dispatches, Parliamentary resolutions; and awakened to find a tall specter grinning and gibbering over the foot of the bed, know that he was there to stay – hadn't they seen the apocalypse as an excuse for a glorious beano, a grand way to see the old century and their respective careers go out?

"You are so like him," the girl was saying, "my uncle Evelyn: tall, and fair, and oh! not really Lardwick-in-the-Fenish at all."

"Haw, haw," Goodfellow replied.

Hearing the languishment in that voice, Porpentine wondered idly if she were bud or bloom; or perhaps a petal blown off and having nothing to belong to anymore. It was difficult to tell – getting more so every year – and he did not know if this were old age beginning to creep up on him at last or some flaw in the generation itself. His own had budded, bloomed, and, sensing some blight in the air, folded its petals up again like certain flowers at sunset. Would it be any use asking her?

"My God," Goodfellow said. They looked up to see an emaciated figure in evening clothes whose head seemed that of a nettled sparrow-hawk. The head guffawed, retaining its fierce expression. Victoria bubbled over in a laugh. "It's Hugh!" she cried, delighted.

"Indeed," echoed a voice inside. "Help me get it off, someone." Porpentine, obliging, stood on a chair to tug off the head.

"Hugh Bongo-Shaftsbury," said Goodfellow, ungracious.

"Harmakhis." Bongo-Shaftsbury indicated the hollow ceramic hawk-head. "God of Heliopolis and chief deity of Lower Egypt. Utterly genuine, this: a mask used in the ancient rituals." He seated himself next to Victoria. Goodfellow scowled. "Literally Horus on the horizon, also represented as a lion with the head of a man. Like the Sphinx."

"Oh," Victoria sighed, "the Sphinx." Enchanted, which did puzzle Porpentine: for this was a violation, was it not, so much rapture over the mongrel gods of Egypt? Her ideal should rightfully have been pure manhood or pure hawkhood; hardly the mixture.

They decided not to have liqueurs but to stay with the Vöslauer, which was off-vintage but only went for ten piastres.

"How far down the Nile do you intend to go?" asked Porpentine. "Mr. Goodfellow has mentioned your interest in Luxor."

"I feel it is fresh territory, sir," replied Bongo-Shaftsbury. "No first-rate work around the area since Grébaut discovered the tomb of the Theban priests back in 'ninety-one. Of course one should have a look round the pyramids at Gizeh, but that is pretty much old hat since Mr. Flinders Petrie's painstaking inspection of sixteen or seventeen years ago."

"I imagine," murmured Porpentine. He could have got the data, of course, from any Baedeker. At least there was a certain intensity or single-minded concern with matters archaeological which Porpentine was sure would drive Sir Alastair to frenzy before the Cook's tour was completed. Unless, like Porpentine and Goodfellow, Bongo-Shaftsbury intended to go no farther than Cairo.

Porpentine hummed the aria from *Manon Lescaut* as Victoria poised prettily between the other two, attempting to keep equilibrium. The crowd in the restaurant had thinned out and across the street the Consulate was dark, save two or three lights in the upstairs rooms. Perhaps in a month all the windows would be blazing; perhaps the world would be blazing. Projected, the courses of Marchand and Kitchener would cross near Fashoda, in the district of Behr el-Abyad, some forty miles above the source of the White Nile. Lord Lansdowne, Secretary of State for War, had predicted 25 September as meeting-date in a secret dispatch to Cairo: a message both Porpentine and Moldweorp had seen. All at once a tic came dancing across Bongo-Shaftsbury's face; there was a time-lag of about five seconds before Porpentine – either intuitively or because of his suspicions about the archaeologist – reckoned who it was that stood behind his chair. Goodfellow nodded, sick and timid; said, civilly enough: "Lepsius, I say. Tired of the climate in Brindisi?" Lepsius. Porpentine hadn't even known the name. Goodfellow would have, of course. "Sudden business called me to Egypt," the agent hissed. Goodfellow sniffed at his wine. Soon: "Your traveling companion? I had rather hoped to see him again."

"Gone to Switzerland," Lepsius said. "The mountains, the clean winds. One can have enough, one day, of the sordidness of that South." They never lied. Who was his new partner?

"Unless you go far enough south," Goodfellow said. "I imagine far enough down the Nile one gets back to a kind of primitive cleanness."

Porpentine had been watching Bongo-Shaftsbury closely, since the tic. The face, lean and ravaged like the body, remained expressionless now; but that initial lapse had set Porpentine on his guard.

"Doesn't the law of the wild beast prevail down there?" Lepsius said. "There are no property rights, only fighting; and the victor wins all. Glory, life, power and property, all."

"Perhaps," Goodfellow said. "But in Europe, you know, we are civilized. Fortunately. Jungle-law is inadmissible."

Soon Lepsius took his leave, expressing the hope they would meet again at Cairo. Goodfellow was certain they would. Bongo-Shaftsbury had continued to sit unmoving and unreadable.

"What a queer gentleman," Victoria said.

"Is it queer," Bongo-Shaftsbury said, deliberately reckless, "to favor the clean over the impure?"

So. Porpentine had wearied of self-congratulation ten years ago. Goodfellow looked embarrassed. So: cleanness. After the deluge, the long famine, the earthquake. A desert-region's cleanness: bleached bones, tombs of dead cultures. Armageddon would sweep the house of Europe so. Did that make Porpentine champion only of cobwebs, rubbish, offscourings? He remembered a night-visit in Rome, years ago, to a contact who lived over a bordello near the Pantheon. Moldweorp himself had followed, taking station near a street-lamp to wait. In the middle of the interview Porpentine chanced to look out the window. A streetwalker was propositioning Moldweorp. They could not hear the conversation, only see a slow and unkind fury recast his features to a wrath-mask; only watch him raise his cane and begin to slash methodically at the girl until she lay ragged at his feet. Porpentine was first to break out of that paralysis, open the door, and race down to the street. When he reached her Moldweorp was gone. His comfort was automatic, perhaps out of some abstract sense of duty, while she screamed into the tweed of his coat. *Mi chiamava sozzura,* she could say: he called me filth. Porpentine had tried to forget the incident. Not because it was ugly but because it showed his terrible flaw so clear: reminding him it was not Moldweorp he hated so much as a perverse idea of what is clean; not the girl he sympathized with so much as her humanity. Fate, it occurred to him then, chooses weird agents. Moldweorp somehow could love and hate individually. The roles being, it seemed, reversed, Porpentine found it necessary to believe if one appointed oneself savior of humanity that perhaps one must love that humanity only in the abstract. For any descent to the personal level can make a purpose less pure. Whereas a disgust at individual human perversity might as easily avalanche into a rage for apocalypse. He could never bring himself to hate the Moldweorp crew, any more than they could avoid genuine anxiety over his welfare. Worse, Porpentine could never make a try for any of them; would remain instead an inept Cremonini singing Des Grieux, expressing certain passions by calculated musical covenant, would never leave a stage where vehemences and tendresses are merely forte and piano, where the Paris gate at Amiens foreshortens mathematically and is illuminated by the precise glow of calcium light. He remembered his performance in the rain that afternoon: he like Victoria needed the proper setting. Anything intensely European, it seemed, inspired him to heights of inanity.

It got late; only two or three tourists left scattered about the room. Victoria showed no signs of fatigue, Goodfellow and Bongo-Shaftsbury argued politics. A waiter lounged two tables away, impatient. He had the delicate build and high narrow skull of the Copt, and Porpentine realized this had been the only non-European in the place, all along. Any such discord should have been spotted immediately: Porpentine's slip. He had no use for Egypt, had sensitive skin and avoided its sun as if any tinge of it might make part of him the East's own. He cared about regions not on the Continent only so far as they might affect its fortunes and no further; the Fink restaurant could as well have been an inferior Voisin's.

At length the party arose, paid, left. Victoria skipped ahead across rue Cherif Pacha to the hotel. Behind them a closed carriage came rattling out of the drive beside the Austrian Consulate and dashed away hell-for-leather down rue de Rosette, into the wet night.

"Someone is in a hurry," Bongo-Shaftsbury noted.

"Indeed," said Goodfellow. To Porpentine: "At the Gare du Caire. The train leaves at eight." Porpentine gave them all good night and returned to his *pied-à-terre* in the Turkish quarter. Such choice of lodgings violated nothing; for he considered the Porte part of the Western World. He fell asleep reading an old and mutilated edition of *Antony and Cleopatra* and wondering if it were still possible to fall under the spell of Egypt: its tropic unreality, its curious gods.

At 7:40 he stood on the platform of the Gare, watching the porters from Cook's and Gaze's pile boxes and trunks. Across the double line of tracks was a small park, green with palms and acacias. Porpentine kept to the shadow of the station-house. Soon the others arrived. He noticed the tiniest flicker of communication pass between Bongo-Shaftsbury and Lepsius. The morning express pulled in, amid sudden commotion on the platform. Porpentine turned to see Lepsius in pursuit of an Arab, who had apparently stolen his valise. Goodfellow had already gone into action. Sprinting across the platform, blond mane flapping wild, he cornered the Arab in a doorway, took back the valise and surrendered his quarry to a fat policeman in a pith helmet. Lepsius watched him snake-eyed and silent as he handed back the valise.

Aboard the train they split up into two adjoining

compartments, Victoria, her father, and Goodfellow sharing the one next the rear platform. Porpentine felt that Sir Alastair would have been less miserable in his company, but wanted to be sure of Bongo-Shaftsbury. The train pulled out at five past eight, heading into the sun. Porpentine leaned back and let Mildred ramble on about mineralogy. Bongo-Shaftsbury kept silent until the train had passed Sidi Gaber and swung toward the southeast.

He said: "Do you play with dolls, Mildred." Porpentine gazed out the window. He felt something unpleasant was about to happen. He could see a procession of dark-colored camels with their drivers, moving slowly along the embankments of a canal. Far down the canal were the small white sails of barges.

"When I'm not out after rocks," said Mildred.

Bongo-Shaftsbury said: "I'll wager you do not have any dolls that walk, or speak, or are able to jump rope. Now do you."

Porpentine tried to concentrate on a group of Arabs who lazed about far down the embankment, evaporating part of the water in Lake Mareotis for salt. The train was going at top speed. He soon lost them in the distance.

"No," said Mildred, doubtful.

Bongo-Shaftsbury said: "But have you never seen dolls like that? Such lovely dolls, and clockwork inside. Dolls that do everything perfectly, because of the machinery. Not like real little boys and girls at all. Real children cry, and act sullen, and won't behave. These dolls are much nicer."

On the right now were fallow cotton-fields and mud huts. Occasionally one of the fellahin would be seen going down to the canal for water. Almost out of his field of vision Porpentine saw Bongo-Shaftsbury's hands, long and starved-nervous, lying still, one on each knee.

"They sound quite nice," said Mildred. Though she knew she was being talked down to her voice was unsteady. Possibly something in the archaeologist's face frightened her.

Bongo-Shaftsbury said: "Would you like to see one, Mildred?" It was going too far. For the man had been talking to Porpentine, the girl was being used. For what? Something was wrong.

"Have you one with you," she wondered, timid. Despite himself Porpentine moved his head away from the window to watch Bongo-Shaftsbury.

Who smiled: "Oh yes." And pushed back the sleeve of his coat to remove a cuff-link. He began to roll back the cuff of his shirt. Then thrust the naked underside of his forearm at the girl. Porpentine recoiled, thinking: Lord love a duck. Bongo-Shaftsbury is insane. Shiny and black against the unsunned flesh was a miniature electric switch, single-pole, double-throw, sewn into the skin. Thin silver wires ran from its terminals up the arm, disappearing under the sleeve.

The young often show a facile acceptance of the horrible. Mildred began to shake. "No," she said, "no: you are not one."

"But I am," protested Bongo-Shaftsbury, smiling, "Mildred. The wires run up into my brain. When the switch is closed like this I act the way I do now. When it is thrown the other – "

The girl shrank away. "Papa," she cried.

"Everything works by electricity," Bongo-Shaftsbury explained, soothing. "And it is simple, and clean."

"Stop it," Porpentine said.

Bongo-Shaftsbury whirled to him. "Why?" he whispered. "Why? For her? Touched by her fright, are you? Or is it for yourself?"

Porpentine retreated, bashful. "One doesn't frighten a child, sir."

"General principles. Damn you." He looked petulant, ready to cry.

There was noise out in the passageway. Goodfellow had been shouting in pain. Porpentine leaped up, shoving Bongo-Shaftsbury aside, and rushed out into the passageway. The door to the rear platform was open: in front of it Goodfellow and an Arab fought, tangled and clawing. Porpentine saw the flash of a pistol-barrel. He moved in cautiously, circling, choosing his point. When the Arab's throat was exposed sufficiently Porpentine kicked, catching him across the windpipe. He collapsed rattling. Goodfellow took the pistol. Pushed back his forelock, sides heaving. "Ta."

"Same one?" Porpentine said.

"No. The railroad police are conscientious. And it is possible, you know, to tell them apart. This is different."

"Cover him, then." To the Arab: *"Auz e. Ma tkhafsh minni."* The Arab's head rolled toward Porpentine, he tried to grin but his eyes were sick. A blue mark was appearing on his throat. He could not talk. Sir Alastair and Victoria had appeared, anxious.

"May have been a friend of the fellow I caught back at the Gare," Goodfellow explained easily. Porpentine helped the Arab to his feet. *"Ruh.* Go back. Don't let us see you again." The Arab moved off.

"You're not going to let him go?" Sir Alastair rumbled. Goodfellow was magnanimous. He gave a short speech about charity and turning the other cheek which was well received by Victoria but which seemed to nauseate her father. The party resumed their places in the compartments, though Mildred had decided to stay with Sir Alastair.

Half an hour later the train pulled into Damanhur. Porpentine saw Lepsius get off two cars ahead and go inside the station-house. Around them stretched the green country of the Delta. Two minutes later the Arab got off and cut across on a diagonal to the buffet entrance; met Lepsius coming out with a bottle of red wine. He was rubbing the mark on his throat and apparently wanted to speak to Lepsius. The agent glared and cuffed him across the head. "No bakshish," he announced. Porpentine settled back, closed his eyes without looking at Bongo-Shaftsbury. Without even saying aha. The train began to move. So. What did they call clean, then? Not observing The Rules, surely. If so they had reversed course. They'd never played so foul before. Could it mean that this meeting at Fashoda would be important: might even be The One? He opened his eyes to watch Bongo-Shaftsbury, engrossed in a book: Sidney J. Webb's *Industrial Democracy*. Porpentine shrugged. Time was his fellow professionals became adept through practice. Learned ciphers by breaking them, customs officials by evading them, some opponents by killing them. Now the new ones read books: young lads, full of theory and (he'd decided) a faith in nothing but the perfection of their own internal machinery. He flinched, remembering the knife-switch, fastened to Bongo-Shaftsbury's arm like a malignant insect. Moldweorp must have been the oldest spy active but in professional ethics he and Porpentine did belong to the same generation. Porpentine doubted if Moldweorp approved of the young man opposite.

Their silence continued for twenty-five miles. The express passed by farms which began to look more and more prosperous, fellahin who worked in the fields at a faster pace, small factories and heaps of ancient ruin and tall flowering tamarisks. The Nile was in flood: stretching away from them, a glittering network of irrigation canals and small basins caught the water, conducted it through wheat and barley fields which extended to the horizon. The train reached the Rosetta arm of the Nile; crossed high over it by a long, narrow iron bridge, entered the station at Kafr ez-Zaiyat, where it stopped. Bongo-Shaftsbury closed the book, arose and left the compartment. A few moments later Goodfellow entered, holding Mildred by the hand.

"He felt you might want to get some sleep," Goodfellow said. "I should have thought. I was preoccupied with Mildred's sister." Porpentine snorted, shut his eyes and fell asleep before the train started to move. He awoke half an hour out of Cairo. "All secure," Goodfellow said. The outlines of the pyramids were visible off to the west. Closer to the city gardens and villas began to appear. The train reached Cairo's Principal Station about noon.

Somehow, Goodfellow and Victoria managed to be in a phaeton and away before the rest of the party got on the platform. "Damme," Sir Alastair puzzled, "what are they doing, eloping?" Bongo-Shaftsbury looked properly outwitted. Porpentine, having slept, felt rather in a holiday mood. *"Arabiyeh,"* he roared, gleeful. A dilapidated pinto-colored barouche came clattering up and Porpentine pointed after the phaeton: "A double piastre if you catch them." The driver grinned; Porpentine hustled everyone into the carriage. Sir Alastair protested, muttering about Mr. Conan Doyle. Bongo-Shaftsbury guffawed and away they galloped, around a sharp curve to the left, over the el-Lemun bridge and pell-mell down Sharia Bab el-Hadid. Mildred made faces at other tourists on foot or riding donkeys, Sir Alastair smiled tentatively. Ahead Porpentine could see Victoria in the phaeton tiny and graceful, holding Goodfellow's arm and leaning back to let the wind blow her hair.

The two carriages arrived at Shepheard's Hotel in a dead heat. All but Porpentine alighted and moved toward the hotel. "Check me in," he called to Goodfellow, "I must see a friend." The friend was a porter at the Hotel Victoria, four blocks south and west. While Porpentine

sat in the kitchen discussing game birds with a mad chef
he had known at Cannes, the porter crossed the street to
the British Consulate, going in by the servants' entrance.
He emerged after fifteen minutes and returned to the
hotel. Soon an order for lunch was brought in to the
kitchen. *Crème"* had been misspelled to read *"chem.";*
"Lyonnaise" was spelled without an *e*. Both were under-
lined. Porpentine nodded, thanked everyone, and left.
He caught a cab and rode up Sharia el-Maghrabi, through
the luxurious park at the end; soon arrived at the Crédit
Lyonnais. Nearby was a small pharmacy. He entered and
asked about the prescription for laudanum he had brought
in to be filled the day before. He was handed an envelope
whose contents, once more in the cab, he checked. A
raise of £50 for him and Goodfellow: good news. They
would both be able to stay at Shepheard's.

Back at the hotel they set about decoding their instructions. F.O. knew nothing about an assassination plot.
Of course not. No reason for one, if you were thinking
only about the immediate question of who would control
the Nile Valley. Porpentine wondered what had happened
to diplomacy. He knew people who had worked under
Palmerston, a shy, humorous old man for whom the
business was a jolly game of blindman's-buff, where every
day one reached out and touched, and was touched by,
the Specter's cold hand.

"We're on our own, then," Goodfellow pointed out.

"Ah," Porpentine agreed. "Suppose we work it this
way: set a thief to catch one. Make plans to do Cromer
in ourselves. Go through the motions only, of course.
That way whenever they get an opportunity, we can be
right on the spot to prevent them."

"Stalk the Consul-General," Goodfellow grew enthusiastic, "like a bloody grouse. Why we haven't done that
since —"

"Never mind," Porpentine said.

That night Porpentine commissioned a cab and roved about the city until early morning. The coded instructions had told them nothing more than to bide time: Goodfellow was taking care of that, having escorted Victoria to an Italian summer-theater performance at the Ezbekiyeh Garden. In the course of the night Porpentine visited a girl who lived in the Quartier Rosetti and was the mistress of a junior clerk in the British Consulate; a jewel merchant in the Muski who had lent financial support to the Mahdists and did not wish now that the movement was crushed to have his sympathies known; a minor Esthetic who had fled England on a narcotics charge to the land of no extradition and who was a distant cousin of the valet to Mr. Raphael Borg, the British Consul; and a pimp named Varkumian who claimed to know every assassin in Cairo. From this fine crew Porpentine returned to his room at three in the morning. But hesitated at the door, having heard movement behind it. Only one thing for it: at the end of the corridor was this window with a ledge outside. He grimaced. But then everyone knew that spies were continually crawling about windowledges, high above the streets of exotic cities. Feeling an utter fool, Porpentine climbed out and got on the ledge. He looked down: there was a drop of about fifteen feet into some bushes. Yawning he made his way quickly but clumsily toward the corner of the building. The ledge became narrower at the corner. As he stood with each foot on a different side and the edge of the building bisecting him from eyebrows to abdomen he lost his balance and fell. On the way down it occurred to him to use an obscene word; he hit the shrubbery with a crash, rolled, and lay there tapping his fingers. After he had smoked half a cigarette he got to his feet and noticed a tree next his own window, easily climbable. He ascended puffing and cursing; crawled out on a limb, straddled it, and peered inside.

Goodfellow and the girl lay on Porpentine's bed, white and exhausted-looking by street-light: her eyes, mouth, and nipples were little dark bruises against the flesh. She cradled Goodfellow's white head in a net or weaving of fingers while he cried, streaking her breasts with tears. "I'm sorry," he was saying, "the Transvaal, a wound. They told me it was not serious." Porpentine, having no idea how this sort of thing worked, fell back on alternatives: (a) Goodfellow was being honorable, (b) was truly impotent and had therefore lied to Porpentine about a long list of conquests, (c) simply had no intention of getting involved with Victoria. Whichever it was, Porpentine felt as always an alien. He swung down by one arm from the limb, nonplused, until the stub of the cigarette burned down to his fingers and made him swear softly; and because he knew it was not really the burn he cursed he began to worry. It was not only seeing Goodfellow weak. He dropped into the bushes and lay there thinking about his own threshold, sustained proudly for twenty years of service. Though it had been hammered at before, he suspected this was the first time it had shown itself truly vulnerable. A pang of superstitious terror caught him flat on his back in the bushes. It seemed he knew, for a space of seconds, that this indeed was The One. Apocalypse would surely begin at Fashoda if for no other reason than that he felt his own so at hand. But soon: gradually, with each lungful of a fresh cigarette's smoke, the old control seeped back to him; and he got at last to his feet, still shaky, walked around to the hotel entrance and up to his room. This time he pretended to've lost his key, making bewildered noises to cover the girl as she gathered her clothing and fled through connecting doors to her own room. All he felt by the time Goodfellow opened was embarrassment, and that he had lived with for a long time.

The theater had presented *Manon Lescaut*. In the shower next morning Goodfellow attempted to sing *"Donna non vidi mai."* "Stop," said Porpentine. "Would you like to hear how it should be done?" Goodfellow howled. "I doubt you could sing Ta-ra-ra-boom-di-ay without mucking it up."

But Porpentine could not resist. He thought it a harmless compromise. *"A dirle io t'amo,"* he caroled, *"a nuova vita l'alma mia si desta."* It was appalling; one got the impression he had once worked in a music-hall. He was no Des Grieux. Des Grieux knows, soon as he sees that young lady just off the diligence from Arras, what will happen. He does not make false starts or feints, this chevalier, has nothing to decode, no double game to play. Porpentine envied him. As he dressed he whistled the aria. Last night's moment of weakness bloomed again behind his eyes. He thought: If I step below the threshold, you know, I shall never get back again.

At two that afternoon the Consul-General emerged from the front door of the Consulate and entered a carriage. Porpentine watched from a deserted room on the third floor of the Hotel Victoria. Lord Cromer was a perfect target but this vantage at least was unavailable to any hired assassin-in-opposition as long as Porpentine's friends kept on the alert. The archaeologist had taken Victoria and Mildred to tour the bazaars and the Tombs of the Khalifs. Goodfellow was sitting in a closed landau directly under the window. Unobtrusive (as Porpentine watched) he started off behind the carriage, keeping at a safe distance. Porpentine left the hotel, strolled up Sharia el-Maghrabi. At the next corner he noticed a church off to his right; heard loud organ music. On a sudden whim he entered the church. Sure enough, it was Sir

Alastair, booming away. It took the unmusical Porpentine some five minutes to come aware of the devastation Sir Alastair was wreaking on the keys and pedals. Music laced the interior of the tiny, Gothic house with certain intricate veinings, weird petal-shapes. But it was violent and somehow Southern foliage. Head and fingers uncontrollable for a neglect of his daughter's or any purity, for the music's own shape, for Bach – was it Bach? – himself? Foreign and a touch shabby, uncomprehending, how could Porpentine say. But was yet unable to pull away until the music stopped abruptly, leaving the church's cavity to reverberate. Only then did he withdraw unseen out into the sun, adjusting his neck-cloth as if it were all the difference between wholeness and disintegration.

Lord Cromer was doing nothing to protect himself, Goodfellow reported that night. Porpentine, having rechecked with the valet's cousin, knew the word had gone through. He shrugged, calling the Consul-General a nitwit; tomorrow was 25 September. He left the hotel at eleven and went by carriage to a *Brauhaus* a few blocks north of the Ezbekiyeh Garden. He sat alone at a small table against the wall, listening to maudlin accordion music which must surely have been old as Bach; closed his eyes, letting a cigarette droop from his lips. A waitress brought Munich beer.

"Mr. Porpentine." He looked up. "I followed you." He nodded, smiled; Victoria sat down. "Papa would die if he ever found out," gazing at him defiant. The accordion stopped. The waitress left two Krugers.

He pursed his lips, ruthful in that quiet. So she'd sought out and found the woman in him; the very first civilian to do so. He did not go through any routine of asking how she knew. She could not have seen him through the window. He said:

"He was sitting in the German church this afternoon,

playing Bach as if it were all he had left. So that he may have guessed."

She hung her head, a mustache of foam on her upper lip. From across the canal came the faint whistle of the express for Alexandria. "You love Goodfellow," he hazarded. Never had he been down so far: he was a tourist here. Could have used, at the moment, any Baedeker of the heart. Almost drowned in a fresh wailing of the accordion her whisper came: yes. Then had Goodfellow told her. . . . He raised his eyebrows, she shook her head no. Amazing, the knowing of one another, these wordless flickerings. "Whatever I may think I have guessed," she said. "Of course you can't trust me, but I have to say it. It's true." How far down could one go, before . . . Desperate. Porpentine: "What do you want me to do, then." She, twisting ringlets round her fingers, would not look at him. Soon: "Nothing. Only understand." If Porpentine had believed in the devil he could have said: you have been sent. Go back and tell him, them, it is no use. The accordionist spotted Porpentine and the girl, recognized them as English. "Had the devil any son," he sang mischievous in German, "it was surely Palmerston." A few Germans laughed, Porpentine winced: the song was fifty years old at least. But a few still remembered.

Varkumian came weaving his way among tables, late. Victoria saw him and excused herself. Varkumian's report was brief: no action. Porpentine sighed. It left only one thing to do. Throw a scare into the Consulate, put them on their guard.

So next day they began "stalking" Cromer in earnest. Porpentine woke up in a foul mood. He donned a red beard and a pearl-gray morning hat and visited the Consulate, posing as an Irish tourist. The staff weren't having any: he got ejected forcibly. Goodfellow had a better idea: "Lob a bomb," he cried. Happily his knowledge of munitions was faulty as his aim. The bomb, instead of falling safely on the lawn, soared in through a window of the Consulate, sending one of the proverbial charwomen into hysterics (though it proved of course to be a dud) and nearly getting Goodfellow arrested.

At noon Porpentine visited the kitchen of the Hotel Victoria to find the place in a turmoil. The meeting at Fashoda had taken place. The Situation had turned to a Crisis. Upset, he dashed out into the street, commandeered a carriage, and tore off in search of Goodfellow. He found him two hours later sleeping in his hotel room where Porpentine had left him. In a rage he emptied a pitcher of ice-water over Goodfellow's head. Bongo-Shaftsbury appeared in the doorway grinning. Porpentine hurled the empty pitcher at him as he vanished down the corridor. "Where's the Consul-General?" Goodfellow inquired, amiable and sleepy. "Get dressed," bellowed Porpentine.

They found the clerk's mistress lying lazy in a patch of sunlight, peeling a mandarin orange. She told them Cromer was planning to attend the opera at eight. Up to then, she could not say. They went to the shop of the chemist, who had nothing for them. Barreling through the Garden Porpentine asked about the Wrens. They were at Heliopolis, as far as Goodfellow knew. "What the bloody hell is wrong with everyone?" Porpentine wanted to know. "Nobody knows anything." They could do nothing till eight; so sat in front of a café in the Garden and drank wine. Egypt's sun beat down, somehow threatening. There was no shade. The fear that had found him night before last now crawled along the flanks of Porpentine's jaw and up his temples. Even Goodfellow seemed nervous.

At a quarter to eight they strolled along the path to the theater, purchased tickets in the orchestra, and settled down to wait. Soon the Consul-General's party arrived and sat near them. Lepsius and Bongo-Shaftsbury drifted in from either side and stationed themselves in boxes; forming, with Lord Cromer as vertex, an angle of 120 degrees. "Bother," said Goodfellow. "We should have got some elevation." Four policemen came marching down the center aisle, glanced up at Bongo-Shaftsbury. He pointed to Porpentine. "My Gawd," Goodfellow moaned. Porpentine closed his eyes. He'd blown it, all right. This was what happened when one blundered right in. The policemen surrounded them, stood at attention. "All right," Porpentine said. He and Goodfellow arose and were escorted out of the theater. "We shall desire your passports," one of them said. Behind them on the breeze came the first sprightly chords of the opening scene. They marched down a narrow path, two police behind, two in front. Signals had, of course, been arranged years before. "I shall want to see the British Consul," Porpentine said and spun, drawing an old single-shot pistol. Goodfellow had the other two covered. The policeman who had asked for their passports glowered. "No one said they would be armed," another protested. Methodically, with four raps to the skull, the policemen were neutralized and rolled into the underbrush. "A fool trick," Goodfellow muttered: "we were lucky." Porpentine was already running back toward the theater. They took the stairs two at a time and searched for an empty box. "Here," Goodfellow said. They edged into the box. It was almost directly across from Bongo-Shaftsbury's. That would put them next to Lepsius. "Keep down," Porpentine said. They crouched, peering between small golden balusters. On stage Edmondo and the students chaffed the Romantic, horny Des Grieux. Bongo-Shaftsbury was checking the action of a small pistol. "Stand by," Goodfellow whispered. The postilion horn of the diligence was heard. The coach came rattling and creaking into the inn courtyard. Bongo-Shaftsbury raised his pistol. Porpentine said: "Lepsius. Next door." Goodfellow withdrew. The diligence bounced to a halt. Porpentine centered his sights on Bongo-Shaftsbury, then let the muzzle drift down and to the right until it pointed at Lord Cromer. It occurred to him that he could end everything for himself right now, never have to worry about Europe again. He had a sick moment of uncertainty. Now how serious had anyone ever been? Was aping Bongo-Shaftsbury's tactics any less real than opposing them? Like a bloody grouse, Goodfellow had said. Manon was helped down from the coach. Des Grieux gaped, was transfixed, read his destiny on her eyes. Someone was standing behind Porpentine. He glanced back, quickly in that moment of hopeless love, and saw Moldweorp there looking decayed, incredibly old, face set in a hideous though compassionate smile. Panicking, Porpentine turned and fired blindly, perhaps at Bongo-Shaftsbury, perhaps at Lord Cromer. He could not see and would never be sure which one he had intended as target. Bongo-Shaftsbury shoved the pistol inside his coat and disappeared. A fight was on out in the corridor. Porpentine pushed the old man aside and ran out in time to see Lepsius tear away from Goodfellow and flee toward the stairs. "Please, dear fellow," Moldweorp gasped. "Don't go after them. You are outnumbered." Porpentine had reached the top step. "Three to two," he muttered.

"More than three. My chief and his, and staff personnel . . ."

Which stopped Porpentine dead. "Your –"

"I have been under orders, you know." The old man sounded apologetic. Then, all in a nostalgic rush: "The Situation, don't you know, it is serious this time, we are all for it – "

Porpentine looked back, exasperated. "Go away," he yelled, "go away and die." And was certain only in a dim way that the interchange of words had now, at last, been decisive.

"The big chief himself," Goodfellow remarked as they ran down the stairs. "Things must be bad." A hundred yards ahead Bongo-Shaftsbury and Lepsius leaped into a carriage. Surprisingly nimble, Moldweorp had taken a short cut. He emerged from an exit to the left of Porpentine and Goodfellow and joined the others. "Let them go," Goodfellow said.

"Are you still taking orders from me?" Without waiting for an answer Porpentine found a phaeton, got in and swung around to pursue. Goodfellow grabbed on and hauled himself up. They galloped down Sharia Kamel Pasha, scattering donkeys, tourists, and dragomans. In front of Shepheard's they nearly ran down Victoria, who had come out into the street. They lost ten seconds while Goodfellow helped her aboard. Porpentine could not protest. Again she had known. Something had passed out of his hands. He was only beginning to recognize, somewhere, a quite enormous betrayal.

It was no longer single combat. Had it ever been? Lepsius, Bongo-Shaftsbury, all the others, had been more than merely tools or physical extensions of Moldweorp. They were all in it; all had a stake, acted as a unit. Under orders. Whose orders? Anything human? He doubted: like a bright hallucination against Cairo's night-sky he saw (it may have been only a line of cloud) a bell-shaped curve, remembered perhaps from some younger F.O. operative's mathematics text. Unlike Constantine on the verge of battle, he could not afford, this late, to be converted at any sign. Only curse himself, silent, for wanting so to believe in a fight according to the duello, even in this period of history. But they – no, it – had not been playing those rules. Only statistical odds. When had he stopped facing an adversary and taken on a Force, a Quantity?

The bell curve is the curve for a normal or Gaussian distribution. An invisible clapper hangs beneath it. Porpentine (though only half-suspecting) was being tolled down.

The carriage ahead took a sharp left, moving toward the canal. There it turned left again, and raced alongside the thin ribbon of water. The moon had risen, half of it, fat and white. "They're going for the Nile Bridge," Goodfellow said. They passed the Khedive's palace and clattered over the bridge. The river flowed dark and viscous under them. On the other side they turned south and sped through moonlight between the Nile and the grounds of the viceregal palace. Ahead the quarry swung right. "Damned if it isn't the road to the pyramids," Goodfellow said. Porpentine nodded; "About five and a half miles." They made the turn and passed the prison and the village of Gizeh, hit a curve, crossed the railroad tracks and headed due west. "Oh," Victoria said quietly, "we're going to see the Sphinx."

"In the moonlight," Goodfellow added, wry. "Leave her alone," Porpentine said. They were silent for the rest of the way, making little gain. Around them irrigation ditches interlaced and sparkled. The two carriages passed fellahin villages and water-wheels. No sound at all in the night save wheels and hoofbeats. And the wind of their passage. As they neared the edge of the desert Goodfellow said, "We're catching up." The road began to slope upward. Protected from the desert by a wall five feet high, it wound around to the left, ascending. Ahead of them suddenly the other carriage lurched and crashed into the wall. The occupants scrambled out and climbed the rest of the way on foot. Porpentine continued on around the curve, stopping about 100 yards from the great pyramid of Kheops. Moldweorp, Lepsius, and Bongo-Shaftsbury were nowhere in sight.

"Let's have a look about," Porpentine said. They rounded the corner of the pyramid. The Sphinx crouched 600 yards to the south. "Damn," Goodfellow said. Victoria pointed. "There," she cried: "going toward the Sphinx." They moved over the rough ground at a dead run. Moldweorp had apparently twisted his ankle. The other two were helping him. Porpentine drew his pistol. "You are for it, old man," he shouted. Bongo-Shaftsbury turned and fired. Goodfellow said: "What are we going to do with them anyway? Let them go." Porpentine did not answer. A moment or so later they brought the Moldweorp agents to bay against the right flank of the great Sphinx.

"Put it down," Bongo-Shaftsbury wheezed. "That is a single-shot, I have a revolver." Porpentine had not reloaded. He shrugged, grinned, tossed the pistol into the sand. Beside him Victoria looked up rapt at the lion, man, or god towering over them. Bongo-Shaftsbury pushed up his shirt-cuff, opened the switch and closed it the other way. A boyish gesture. Lepsius stood in the shadows, Moldweorp smiled. "Now," Bongo-Shaftsbury said. "Let them go," Porpentine said. Bongo-Shaftsbury nodded. "It is no concern of theirs," he agreed. "This is between you and the Chief, is it not?" Ho, ho, thought Porpentine: couldn't it have been? Like Des Grieux he must have his delusion even now; could never admit himself entirely a gull. Goodfellow took Victoria's hand and they moved away, back toward the carriage, the girl gazing back restless, eyes glowing at the Sphinx.

"You screamed at the Chief," Bongo-Shaftsbury announced. "You said: Go away and die."

Porpentine put his hands behind his back. Of course.

Had they been waiting for this, then? For fifteen years? He'd crossed some threshold without knowing. Mongrel now, no longer pure. He turned to watch Victoria move away, all tender and winsome for her Sphinx. Mongrel, he supposed, is only another way of saying human. After the final step you could not, nothing could be, clean. It was almost as if they'd tried for Goodfellow because he had stepped below the threshold that morning at the Gare du Caire. Now Porpentine had performed his own fatal act of love or charity by screaming at the Chief. And found out, shortly after, what he'd really screamed at. The two – act and betrayal – canceled out. Canceled to zero. Did they always? Oh God. He turned again to Moldweorp.

His Manon?

"You have been good enemies," he said at last. It sounded wrong to him. Perhaps if there had been more time, time to learn the new role . . .

It was all they needed. Goodfellow heard the shot, turned in time to see Porpentine fall to the sand. He cried out; watched the three turn and move away. Perhaps they would walk straight out into the Libyan desert and keep walking till they reached the shore of some sea. Soon he turned to the girl, shaking his head. He took her hand and they went to find the phaeton. Sixteen years later, of course, he was in Sarajevo, loitering among crowds assembled to greet the Archduke Francis Ferdinand. Rumors of an assassination, a possible spark to apocalypse. He must be there to prevent it if he could. His body had become stooped and much of his hair had fallen out. From time to time he squeezed the hand of his latest conquest, a blonde barmaid with a mustache who described him to her friends as a simple-minded Englishman, not much good in bed but liberal with his money.

THE SECRET
INTEGRATION

OUTSIDE it was raining, the first rain of October, end of haying season and of the fall's brilliance, purity of light, a certain soundness to weather that had brought New Yorkers flooding up through the Berkshires not too many weekends ago to see the trees changing in that sun. Today, by contrast, it was Saturday and raining, a lousy combination. Inside at the moment was Tim Santora, waiting for ten o'clock and wondering how he was going to get out past his mother. Grover wanted to see him at ten this morning, so he had to go. He sat curled in an old washing machine that lay on its side in a back room of the house; he listened to rain going down a drainpipe and looked at a wart that was on his finger. The wart had been there for two weeks and wasn't going to go away. The other day his mother had taken him over to Doctor Slothrop, who painted some red stuff on it, turned out the lights and said, "Now, when I switch on my magic purple lamp, watch what happens to the wart." It wasn't a very magic-looking lamp, but when the doctor turned it on, the wart glowed a bright green.

"Ah, good," said Doctor Slothrop. "Green. That means the wart will go away, Tim. It hasn't got a chance." But as they were going out, the doctor said to Tim's mother, in a lowered voice Tim had learned how to listen in on, "Suggestion therapy works about half the time. If this doesn't clear up now spontaneously, bring him back and we'll try liquid nitrogen." Soon as he got home, Tim ran over to ask Grover what "suggestion therapy" meant. He found him down in the cellar, working on another invention.

Grover Snodd was a little older than Tim, and a boy genius. Within limits, anyway. A boy genius with flaws. His inventions, for example, didn't always work. And last year he'd had this racket, doing everybody's homework for them at a dime an assignment. But he'd given himself away too often. They knew somehow (they had a "curve," according to Grover, that told them how well everybody was supposed to do) that it was him behind all the 90s and 100s kids started getting. "You can't fight the law of averages," Grover said, "you can't fight the curve." So they went to work earnestly on his parents to talk them into transferring him. Someplace. Anyplace. Expert though he might be on every school topic from igneous rocks to Indian raids, Grover was still too dumb, as Tim saw it, to cover up how smart he was. Whenever he had a chance to show it, he'd always weaken. In a problem like somebody's yard's a triangle, find the area, Grover couldn't resist bringing in a little trigonometry, which half the class couldn't even pronounce, or calculus, a word they saw from time to time in the outer-space comics and was only a word. But Tim and others were tolerant about it. Why shouldn't Grover show off? He had a hard time sometimes. It wasn't any use talking to people his own age about higher mathematics or higher anything else. He used to discuss foreign policy with his father, Grover confided to Tim, until one night they'd had a serious division of views over Berlin. "I know what they ought to do," Grover yelled (he always yelled – at walls, at anything else solid that happened to be around – to let you know it wasn't you he was mad at but some-thing else, something to do with the scaled-up world adults made, remade and lived in without him, some inertia and stubbornness he was too small, except inside himself, to overcome), "exactly what they should do." But when Tim asked what, Grover only said, "Never mind. The thing we argued about isn't important. But now we don't talk; that *is* important. When I'm home now they let me alone and I let them alone." This year he was only home on weekends and Wednesdays. Other days he commuted twenty miles to college, a Berkshire men's college patterned on Williams but smaller, to take courses and talk to people about higher everything. The public school had won, had banished him. They didn't have time for him, and wanted everybody doing their own homework. It was apparently OK with Grover's father too, because of that estrangement over Berlin. "It isn't that he's stupid, or mean," Grover yelled at his family's oil burner. "He isn't. It's worse than that. He understands things that I don't care about. And I care about things he'll never understand."

"I don't get it," said Tim. "Hey, Grover, what's 'sug-gestion therapy' mean?"

"Like faith healing," said Grover. "That how they're trying to get rid of that wart?"

"Yeah." He told about the red stuff that glowed green, and the lamp.

"Ultraviolet fluorescence," Grover said, having obvious fun with the words, "has no effect on the wart. They're trying to talk it away, but I just messed that up for them," and he started laughing, rolling around on the floor of the cellar, as if somebody was tickling him. "It won't work. When it wants to go away, it will, that's all. Warts have a mind of their own."

It tickled Grover any time he could interfere with the scheming of grownups. It never occurred to Tim to want to figure out why this was so. Grover himself cared only slightly about his own motives. "They think I'm smarter than I am," he hazarded once. "They have this idea about a 'boy genius,' I think – what one is supposed to be, you know. They see them on television or something, and that's what they want me to be like." He'd been very mad that day, Tim remembered, because a new invention hadn't worked out. A sodium grenade: two compartments, sodium and water, separated by a burst-diaphragm. When the sodium came in contact with the water, it would go off with a tremendous bang. But the diaphragm was too strong or something, and it wouldn't break. To make things worse, Grover had been reading *Tom Swift and His Wizard Camera,* by Victor Appleton. He kept coming across these Tom Swift books by apparent accident, though he had developed the theory lately that it was by design; that the books were coming across *him,* and that his parents and/or the school were deeply in-volved. Tom Swift books were a direct affront to him, as if he were expected to compete, to build even better inventions and make even more money on them and invest it more wisely than Tom Swift.

"I hate Tom Swift!" he yelled.

"Quit reading those books, then," Tim suggested.

But Grover couldn't; he tried, but he couldn't stop. Every time one of them popped up, as if from an invisible, malevolent toaster, he'd devour it. It was an addiction; he was haunted by Aerial Warships, Electric Rifles. "It's awful," he said, "the guy's a show-off, he talks funny, and he's a snob, and" – hitting his head to remember the word – "a racist."

"A what?"

"You know this colored servant Tom Swift has, remember, named Eradicate Sampson? Rad for short. The way he treats that guy, it's disgusting. Do they want me to read that stuff so I'll be like that?"

"Maybe that's how," said Tim, excited, having figured it out all at once, "how they want you to be with Carl." He meant Carl Barrington, a colored kid they knew. His family had moved here from Pittsfield not so long ago. The Barringtons lived in Northumberland Estates, a new development out across an abandoned quarry and a couple of rye fields from the older part of Mingeborough that Grover and Tim lived in. Like them, and Étienne Cherdlu, Carl was a nut for practical jokes, not just watching and laughing, but for actually playing them and thinking up new ones, this being one reason the four of them hung around together. The suggestion that Rad, a character in a book, had anything to do with Carl puzzled Grover.

"Don't they like Carl, or what?" he said.

"I don't think it's him. It's his mother and father."

"What did they do?"

Tim made a don't-ask-me face. "Pittsfield is a city," he said. "I guess you can do almost anything in a city. Maybe they ran a numbers game."

"You got that from watching television," Grover accused, and Tim said yeah and laughed. Grover said, "Does your mother know that you and me and Carl go out – you know – fool around?"

"I didn't tell her," Tim said. "She didn't say not to."

"Don't tell her," said Grover. Tim didn't. It wasn't that Grover ever gave orders, but there was an understanding among all of them that even though sometimes he was wrong about things, he still knew more than any of the rest of them and they ought to listen to him. If he told you that a wart wasn't going to go away, that it had a mind of its own, all the purple lights and green fluorescence in Massachusetts would not prevail. The wart would stay.

Tim looked at the wart, a little leery about it, as if it did have a separate intelligence. If he'd been a few years younger, he would have given the wart a name, but he was beginning to realize only little kids named things. Now he sat inside the washing machine he'd used last year for a space capsule, listened to the rain, began to think of getting old, and then older and older without bound, cut the thought off before it modulated to the matter of dying, decided to ask Grover today if he'd learned anything new about the other thing, the liquid nitrogen. "Nitrogen is a gas," Grover had told him, "I never heard of it being a liquid." That was all. But he might have something today. You never knew what he was going to come back from college with. Once he'd brought a multicolored model of a protein molecule, which was now in the hideout, along with the Japanese TV and the sodium stockpile, a bunch of old transmission parts from Étienne Cherdlu's father's junkyard, concrete bust of Alf Landon stolen in one of the weekly raids on Mingeborough Park, busted Mies van der Rohe chair salvaged from another of the old estates, not to mention assorted chandelier pieces, fragments of tapestries, teak newels, one fur overcoat they could hang around the neck of the bust and hide under sometimes, like in a tent.

Tim rolled out of the machine and went as quietly as he could into the kitchen to check the clock. It was a little past ten. Grover was never on time himself, but he always wanted other people to be. "Punctuality," he would declaim, rolling the word at you like an invincible purey, "is not one of your salient virtues." All you had to say to him then was "Huh?" and he'd forget it and get down to business. One of the reasons Tim liked him.

Tim's mother wasn't in the living room, the television was off, and at first he thought she might have gone out. He pulled his raincoat down off the hanger in the hall closet and started for the back door. Then he heard her dialing. He came around a corner, and there she was under the back stairs, holding the blue Princess telephone between her jaw and shoulder. She'd been dialing with one hand and holding the other in front of her in a tight, pale fist. There was a look on her face Tim had never seen before. A little – what do you call it, nervous? scared? – he didn't know. If she saw him there she gave no sign, though he'd made noise enough. The receiver stopped buzzing, and somebody answered.

"You niggers," his mother spat out suddenly, "dirty niggers, get out of this town, go back to Pittsfield. Get out before you get in real trouble." Then she hung up fast. The hand that was in a fist had been shaking, and now her other hand, once it let go of the receiver, started shaking a little too. She turned swiftly, as if she'd smelled him like a deer; caught Tim looking at her in astonishment.

"Oh, you," she said, beginning to smile, except for her eyes.

"What were you doing?" Tim said, which wasn't what he'd meant to ask.

"Oh, playing a joke, Tim," she said, "a practical joke."

Tim shrugged and went on out the back door. "I'm going out," he told her, without looking back. He knew she wouldn't give him any trouble now about it, because he'd caught her.

He ran out into the rain and past two wet lilac bushes, down a slope into long grass turned to hay, his sneakers soaked after only a couple-three steps. Grover Snodd's house, an older one than Tim's with a gambrel roof, edged out from behind a big maple to greet him. When he'd been younger Tim used to think of the house as a person, and say hello to it each time he came over, as if it actually were peeking around the maple at him, friendly, in a kind of game between friends. He still was not at the point where he could give this up completely; it would be cruel to the house to stop believing in it. So: "Hi, house," he said, as usual. The house had a face on the end, a pleasant old face, windows for eyes and nose, a face that always seemed to be smiling. Tim ran on by it, for just a moment only a shadow, dwarfed against the towering, benevolent face. The rain was coming down pretty hard. He skidded around a corner and up to another maple with pieces of board nailed to the side of the trunk. Up, slipping once, and out a long limb to Grover's window. Whistling, electronic sounds came from inside. "Grovie," Tim said, banging on the window. "Hey."

Grover opened the window and announced to Tim that he had a lamentable tendency to dilatoriness.

"Wha?" said Tim.

"I just heard a kid in New York," Grover told him as Tim climbed into the room. "There's something funny with the sky today, because – you know – I have trouble most of the time just getting Springfield." Grover was a radio ham. He put together his own transceiver rigs and test equipment. Not only the sky but these mountains, too, made incoming signals capricious. Grover's room, certain nights when Tim stayed over, filled as the hour grew late with disembodied voices, sometimes even from as far away as the sea. Grover liked to listen but he seldom transmitted to anybody. He had road maps stuck up on the wall and each time he heard a new voice he'd mark it

[*148*]

on the map, along with the frequency. Tim had never seen him sleep. He'd still be up no matter what time Tim turned in, fooling with dials, pressing a huge pair of rubber earphones to his head. There was a speaker too; sometimes he had that on. Drifting in and out of sleep, Tim would hear, mixed with dreams, cops being called to investigate car wrecks or just noises or shadows that moved where everything should have been still, cabbies out to meet the night's trains and grouching mostly about coffee or cracking dry jokes with their dispatcher, some half of a chess game, tugs across the Dutch Hills taking a string of gravel barges down the Hudson, road workers in the autumn and winter working late getting out snow fence or plowing, a merchantman at sea now and then when the thing in the sky, the Heaviside layer, was right for it – all these coming down, filtering through to populate his dreams, so that in the morning he'd never know which had been real, which he'd hallucinated. Grover never was any help. Waking up, before he was fully out of dreams, Tim would say, "Grovie, what about the lost raccoon? The cops find him?" or, "What about that Canadian logger in the houseboat up the river?" And Grover would always answer, "I don't remember that." When Étienne Cherdlu stayed over too, he'd remember different things than Tim did: singing, or badger-watchers reporting in to some kind of headquarters, or bitter arguments, half in Italian, about pro football.

Étienne was supposed to be here today too. It was a regular Saturday-morning briefing session. Probably his father had kept him late again working over at the junkyard. He was a very fat kid who wrote his name "80N," usually on telephone poles with "ha, ha" after it, in crayon, yellow keel swiped from road crews. Like Tim and Grover and Carl, Étienne loved to play practical jokes, only with him it was an obsession. Grover was a genius, Tim wanted someday to become a basketball coach, Carl might star on one of his teams, but Étienne, all he could see was a career somehow playing jokes. "That's crazy," kids would tell him. "A career? You mean a comedian or something on TV, a clown, what?" And Étienne, putting his arm around your shoulders (which, if you were alert enough, you realized he was doing not out of friendship but to Scotch-tape a sign to you reading MY MOTHER WEARS COMBAT BOOTS, or KICK HERE, with an arrow), would tell you, "My father says everything's going to be machines when we grow up. He says the only jobs open will be in junkyards for busted machines. The only thing a machine *can't* do is play jokes. That's all they'll use people for, is jokes."

The kids might have been right: maybe he was a little crazy. He took chances nobody else would, letting air out of tires on cop cars, putting on skin-diving gear to stir up silt in the creek the paper mill used (which once stopped production for nearly a week), leaving silly and almost meaningless notes signed "The Phantom" on the principal's desk while she was out of her office teaching eighth grade – stuff like that. He hated institutions. His great enemies, his jokes' perpetual targets, were the school, the railroad, the PTA. He had gathered around him a discontented bunch the principal, when she was yelling at them, never failed to call "uneducable," a word none of them understood and which Grover wouldn't explain to them because it made him mad, it was like calling somebody a wop, or a nigger. Étienne's friends included the Mostly brothers, Arnold and Kermit, who sniffed airplane glue and stole mousetraps from the store, which for fun they would then cock, stand out in the middle of some empty field and throw at each other; Kim Dufay, a slender, exotic-looking sixth-grader with a blond pigtail that hung to her waist and was usually blue on the end from being dunked in inkwells, who had a thing about explosive chemical reactions and was responsible for replenishing the cache of sodium up at the hideout, smuggling the stuff out of the Mingeborough High School lab with the connivance of her boyfriend Gaylord, an infatuated sophomore shot-putter who just liked them young; Hogan Slothrop, the doctor's kid, who at the age of eight had taken to serious after-bedtime beer-drinking and at the age of nine got religion, swore off beer and joined the Alcoholics Anonymous, a step his father, who was what is known as permissive, gave his blessing to and which the local A.A. group tolerated because they thought having a kid around would be inspirational; Nunzi Passarella, who had begun his career in second grade by bringing somehow a full-grown pig in to Show-and-Tell Time, a quarter-ton Poland China sow, in the school bus and everything, and had gone on to found a Crazy Sue Dunham cult, in honor of that legendary and beautiful drifter who last century had roamed all this hilltop country exchanging babies and setting fires and who, in a way, was the patron saint of all these kids.

"Where's Carl?" Tim said after drying his head on one of Grover's sweat shirts.

"Down cellar," Grover said, "fooling with the rhinoceros feet." Which you could wear like shoes and which would be worn so come the first snowfall. "What's the matter?"

"My mother's been" – he had a hard time saying it because you were not supposed to tell on your mother – "bothering people. Again."

"Bothering Carl's folks?"

Tim nodded.

Grover frowned. "My mother has, too. I hear them talking about it, you know" – making a thumb at a pair of earphones running in a direct line off a bug he'd had planted for a year in his parents' bedroom – "it's called the race issue. For a long time I thought they meant a real race, cars or something."

"And she used that word again," Tim said. At which point Carl came in, without the rhinoceros feet, smiling and quiet, as if he'd had some kind of a bug on Grover's room too and knew what they'd been talking about.

"You want to listen?" Grover said, nodding at the ham equipment. "I had New York for a minute."

Carl said yeah, went over and put on the earphones and started tuning.

"Here's Étienne," said Tim. The fat boy hovered at the window like a slick balloon. He had grease on his face and was making cross-eyes. They let him in. "I got something you'll get a real bang out of," Étienne said.

"What?" said Tim, who was still half thinking about his mother and was not too alert.

"This," said Étienne, and socked him with a paper bag full of rain water he'd been hiding in his shirt. Tim grabbed him and they wrestled around, Grover yelling at them to be careful of the radio gear, Carl lifting his feet and laughing whenever they rolled close. When they quit, Carl took off the earphones and hit the power switch and Grovie went to sit cross-legged on the bed, which meant the Inner Junta was in session.

"Progress reports first, I think," said Grover. "What have you got this week, Étienne?" He had this clipboard he always would snap the clip of rhythmically whenever he was thinking hard.

Étienne took out some papers he had folded in his back pocket and read, "Railroad. One new lantern, two torpedoes added to the arsenic."

"Arsenal," muttered Grover, writing on the clipboard.

"Yeah. Me and Kermie went out and did another count on cars at points Foxtrot and Quebec. Foxtrot showed seventeen cars, three trucks between four-thirty and — "

"I'll take the figures later," Grover said. "Can we do anything in that cut, on that stretch of track, then, or do too many cars come by up on the road? – that's the point."

"Oh," said Étienne. "Well, it was pretty heavy traffic, Grovie." He stuck his teeth out and did slant-eyes at Carl and Tim, who started laughing.

"Can you get out any later?" Grover said irritably. "Later at night, say about nine?"

"I don't know," said Étienne. "I'd have to sneak out and – "

"Well, sneak out," Grover said. "We need figures for the night, too."

"But he – he worries about me," Étienne said, "he really does."

Grover frowned at his clipboard, snapped the clip a couple of times, and said, "Well, how about the school? Anything on that?"

"I have a couple of more little kids lined up," Étienne said, "first-graders. They're always getting yelled at. They throw chalk. They throw anything. One of them has a real good arm, Grovie. We'd have to drill them a little with the sodium. That might be a problem."

Grover looked up. "Problem?"

"They might try to eat it or something. One of them" – giggling – "chews chalk. He says it tastes good."

"Well," said Grover, "keep looking. We need somebody, Étienne. It's a very vital area. We're going to *have* to demolish that boys' latrine. It's symmetry we're after."

"Cemetery?" said Tim, squinting his eyes and wrinkling his nose. "What do you want the cemetery for, Grovie?"

Grover explained the word to him. Sketched a rough plan view of the school building with chalk on his green-board on the wall. "Symmetry and timing," he yelled, "coordination."

"That's on my report card," said Étienne, "that word."

"Right," said Grover. "It means your arms and legs and head all work together in gym, and it's the same for us, in this thing, for a gang like ours, as it is for the parts of your body," but they'd quit listening. Étienne was pulling his mouth wide; Tim and Carl were taking turns socking each other in the arm. Grover snapped his clipboard real loud at them and they quit fooling around. "Étienne, anything more?"

"That's all. Oh, the PTA meeting Tuesday. I think I'll send Hogan again."

"You remember last time," Grover said with an effort, "what he did." The original idea had been that Hogan Slothrop would make a better infiltrator into the PTA meetings because of his experience with Alcoholics Anonymous, Grover's assumption being that Hogan knew most about the kinds of meetings grownups had. It was another miscalculation. It bothered Grover for a week that he'd judged things so wrong. What Hogan had tried to do, instead of just sit quiet, out of sight, taking notes, was horn in on one meeting. "I mean," said Hogan, "I didn't see any harm in raising my hand, you know, and saying, 'My name is Hogan Slothrop, I am a school kid,' and then telling them what it was like."

"They don't want to know," said Grover.

"My mother does," Hogan said. "She asks me every day what I did in school, and I tell her."

"She doesn't listen," said Grover. They had thrown Hogan Slothrop out of the PTA meeting about the time he started up front to the podium to see if they'd let him recite the A.A.'s Twelve Steps. Literally threw him out — he was light and easy to lift.

"Why?" Grover screamed.

"There are meetings," Hogan tried to explain, "and meetings. The PTA does it all different. They have these rules, or something, and everybody is more, more . . . "

"Formal," suggested Grover. "Official."

"Like they're playing some game, a new one I never heard of before," Hogan said. "At the A.A. we just talk."

Next PTA meeting Kim Dufay put on lipstick, did her hair in a French twist, dolled up in her most sophisticated clothes and a size 28A padded bra she'd conned her mother into buying her, and went in and did a pretty good job of passing. So she'd become the new infiltrator.

"And now," Étienne summarized, "Hogan feels bad about being replaced by a girl."

"I like Hogan," Grover said, "don't get me wrong, fellas. But can he function well in a highly structured situation, that's what I – "

"Wha?" said Tim and Carl in unison. It was a bit they'd worked up between them and it never failed to confound Grover. Grover shrugged, admitted there might be a morale problem and told Étienne OK, Hogan could try it again. Tim's report was next. His area of concern was money and drilling. At the moment everybody was occupied with the yearly dry run coming up. The code name for it was Operation Spartacus, which Grover had taken from the movie of the same name, having gone all the way over to Stockbridge one time to see it and been so impressed that for the month following he couldn't go by a mirror without making a Kirk Douglas face at himself in it. This would be the third year for Spartacus, the third dry run for the real uprising of the slaves, referred to only as Operation A. "What's the A for?" Tim had asked once. "Abattoir," Grover answered with a funny look. "Armageddon." "Show-off," Tim said, and forgot it. You didn't have to know what initials meant to drill kids.

"How's it shaping up, Tim?" asked Grover.

Tim wasn't too enthusiastic. "Without a good mock-up, Grovie, it just won't be worth much."

"Just to recap for the others now, Tim," Grover said, writing on the clipboard, "we're handling it more or less the same as last year, right?"

"Right. Using Fazzo's Field again and laying it down" – pointing at the sketch on the greenboard – "full size. But we're using the little stakes and red flags that Étienne got from the road crew this year instead of the lime." Last year too many little kids had been doing just great up until they got to the white outline of the school building, then they'd stopped short and stood around scuffing it into the grass with their shoes. In the critique held later Grover advanced the theory that the line figure in the grass might have reminded the little kids of chalk lines on a greenboard. With the lime there'd also been the problem of getting the thing erased when Spartacus was over. But stakes, them you could just pull up. Stakes were better.

"But not," said Tim, "still not as good as real walls. Even beaver board ones. Running across a line, making believe it's a door, that's one thing. But you need the door itself. You need real stairs, and real toilets to throw the sodium in, you know?"

"But two years ago you didn't feel that way," Grover pointed out.

Tim shrugged. "It just isn't that real anymore. For me. How do we know, when it's time, zero hour, that they'll do it the same way? Especially the little kids?"

"We don't," said Grover. "But we can't afford to build any real elaborate mock-up."

"We have about twenty-five bucks," Tim said. "They're really starting to come through with their milk money now, even some of the ones who, it isn't their turn, you know?"

Grover gave him a lidded look. "You been strong-arming them, Tim? I don't need any of that."

"No, Grovie, I swear, they're all doing it on their own. They say — a couple kids did — that they *believe* in us. Some of them don't like milk anyway, so they don't mind passing it up."

"Just see that they don't get too enthusiastic," Grover said. "The teachers might catch on. The idea is to have a more or less constant milk count every day, to rotate it, very gradually, very quietly. The daily take may be small that way but it's steady. You start getting these wild fluctuations, everybody handing you nickels at once, they'll get suspicious. Go easy. How's the other income? How's our fence in Pittsfield?"

"He wants furniture now," Tim said. "That's a problem. We can get furniture, from the Velour estate, from the Rosenzweig place, from two or three others. But how do we carry it to Pittsfield? We can't. And he's also quit accepting collect calls."

"Gah," said Grover, "then we might as well cross him off too. See? You can't trust them. They start going cheap on you and that means they don't want you around anymore."

"Uh, how about," Tim put in, trying to keep Grover from getting started, "you know, that mock-up?"

"No, no," Grover said. "We need that money for other things." Tim flopped back on the rug and looked at the ceiling. "That's all, Tim? OK, Carl now. How's it going up the development?"

Carl was their organizer for all Northumberland Estates, the new part of Mingeborough. The old town would be easy enough to handle when it was time, but this development shopping center with its supermarket and bright new drugstore that sold Halloween masks, and parking lot always full of cars, even late into the night, bothered them. While it was being put up, the summer before last, Tim and Étienne used to go there evenings and play

king-of-the-mountain on the piles of fill till it was dark;
then they'd steal lumber, drain the gas tanks of graders
and bulldozers, even bust a few windows if the peepers
and frogs in Corrody's Swamp down the hill were singing
loud enough. The kids didn't like the development much,
didn't like it being called "estates" when each lot was
only fifty by a hundred feet, nowhere near the size of the
old Gilded Age estates, real ones, that surrounded the
old town the way creatures in dreams surround your bed,
higher and hidden but always there. Like Grover's house,
the Big Houses of the estates also had faces, but without
such plain, gambreled honesty: Instead there were mys-
terious deep eyes fringed in gimcrackery and wrought-
iron masks, cheeks tattooed in flowered tiles, great port-
cullised mouths with rows of dead palm trees for teeth,
and to visit one of them was like reentering sleep, and
the loot you came away with did not ever seem that real;
whether you kept it to furnish the hideout with, or sold
it to a fence like this antique shop in Pittsfield, it was
the spoils of dream. But there was nothing about the
little, low-rambling, more or less identical homes of
Northumberland Estates to interest or to haunt, no
chance of loot that would be any more than the ordinary,
waking-world kind the cops hauled you in for taking;
no small immunities, no possibilities for hidden life or
otherworldly presence; no trees, secret routes, shortcuts,
culverts, thickets that could be made hollow in the
middle – everything in the place was out in the open,
everything could be seen at a glance; and behind it,
under it, around the corners of its houses and down the
safe, gentle curves of its streets, you came back, you kept
coming back, to nothing; nothing but the cheerless earth.
Carl was one of the few kids who lived there that the
old-town kids could get along with. It was his job to
drum up support, to win new converts, to scout out any

strategic importance there might be to crossroads, stores, things like that. It wasn't a job the others envied him.

"There've been these phone calls," Carl mentioned, after he'd given a rundown on how his week had gone. "Practical jokers." He told some of the things they'd said.

"Jokes," Étienne said. "What's so funny? Call somebody up, call them names, that isn't a joke. It doesn't make any sense at all."

"What about it, Carl?" Grover wanted to know. "Think they suspect anything? Think they caught on what we're up to?"

Carl smiled and so they knew what he was going to say. "No, it's safe. Still safe."

"Then why the phone calls?" Grover said. "If not Operation A, then what?"

Carl shrugged and sat watching them, as if he knew what, knew everything, secrets none of them had even guessed at. As if there were after all some heart-in-hiding, some crypt to Northumberland Estates that had so far managed to elude the rest of them, and which Carl would only someday tell them about, as reward for their having been more ingenious in their scheming, or braver in facing up to their parents, or smarter in school, or maybe better in some way they hadn't yet considered but which Carl would let them know about when he was ready, through hints, funny stories, apparently casual changes of subject.

"End of the meeting," Grover announced. "Let's go over to the hideout."

The rain had fallen away to a sort of drifting mist. The four of them scrambled down the tree and ran out of Grover's yard, down the block, into and across a field among rain-flattened holidays of hay. Somewhere en route they picked up a fat basset hound named Pierre, who on sunny days slept in the middle of the state highway that briefly became Chickadee Street as it passed through Mingeborough. But rain did something to him, invigorated him. He romped around them like a puppy, yapping and trying, it looked like, to catch raindrops on his tongue.

The sun would set tonight without anyone's seeing it – there was that kind of bleakness to the afternoon. You couldn't see any mountains because the clouds trailed too low. Tim, Grover, Étienne, Carl and Pierre went flickering over the field like shadows, out to a dirt road whose ruts were filled with rain now. The road wound down a little ridge into King Yrjö's woods, named after a European pretender who'd fled the eclipse then falling over Europe and his own hardly real shadow-state sometime back in the middle Thirties, trading a bucketful of jewels, the yarn went, for all this property. Why it had to be a bucketful, which sounded like an impractical way to carry jewels around, nobody ever explained. There were also supposed to have been three (some said four) wives, one official and the others morganatic, and a fiercely loyal aide, a cavalry officer seven feet tall with a full beard, spurred boots, gold epaulets and a shotgun he always carried with him and would not hesitate to use on anybody, especially a kid, caught trespassing. It was he who haunted the grounds. He still lived there though his king had long gone – at least, everybody believed he did – though no one had ever seen him outright, only heard his heavy boots crashing after you through the dead leaves, among the tree trunks and briers, as you ran in panic. You always got away. The king's exile, kids could sense, was something their parents were in on but was effectively cut off from the kids: There had been the falling dark, yes, and general flight, and a large war – all this without names and dates, pieced together out of talk overheard from parents, television documentaries, social-studies class if you happened to be listening, marines-in-action comics, but none of it that sharp, that specific; all of it in a kind of code, twilit, forever unexplained. King Yrjö's estate was the only real connection the kids had with whatever the cataclysmic thing was that had happened, and it helped for the caretaker, the pursuer, to have been a soldier.

Yet he had not bothered the Inner Junta at all. Years ago, somehow, it had become clear to only them that he never would. They'd since been all over the place and had seen no definite trace of him, though plenty of ambiguous ones. Which didn't disprove his existence, but did mean that they'd found the perfect place for a hideout. Real or make-believe, the giant cavalryman became their protector.

The road passed through a stand of pines, high in whose branches partridges whirred. Water dripped; shoes squished in the mud. After the trees came a sweep of what had once been smooth lawn, smooth as the back of a long wave out at sea, but now was full of weeds, rabbit holes, tall rye. According to Tim's father, years ago peacocks had come running downhill across the great lawn whenever a carriage had entered this stretch of the road, spreading out their brilliant tails. "Oh, yeah," Tim said, "like just before a program comes on in color. When are we getting a color TV, Dad?"

"Black and white's good enough," his father had said, and that was that. Tim had asked Carl once whether he had a color TV at home. "Why should I?" said Carl, and then almost immediately, "Oh! yeah." And bust out laughing. Tim knew as well as Étienne, the professional comic, when your listener had guessed your next line, so he didn't say anything else. He wondered why Carl laughed so hard. It wasn't that funny and even had a kind of logic to it. He did think of Carl as not only "colored" himself, but somehow more deeply involved with *all* color. When Tim thought about Carl he always saw him against blazing reds and ochres of this early fall, only last month, when Carl had just come to Minge-borough and they were still getting to be friends, and he thought that Carl must somehow carry around with him a perpetual Berkshire autumn, a Wonderful World of Color. Even in the grayness of this afternoon and this district they had entered (which, it seemed, was deprived of its just measure of light because part of it belonged to the past), Carl brought a kind of illumination, a brightening, a compensation for whatever it was about the light that was missing.

They left the road and plunged down through azalea bushes to the banks of an ornamental canal, part of a system of waterways and islands laid out toward the end of the last century, perhaps with some idea of a miniaturized or toy Venice for the New York candy magnate Ellsworth Baffy, who had caused this place to be built originally. Like many who put castles up among these inland hills, he was a contemporary of Jay Gould and his partner, the jolly Berkshire peddler Jubilee Jim Fisk. Once, right around this time of year, Baffy had held a masquerade ball in honor of the presidential candidate James G. Blaine, from which Blaine had been absent due to a storm and a mix-up in rail schedules. No one missed him. All the moneyed of Berkshire County congregated in the great ballroom of Baffy's spun-sugar manor house; the party lasted three days and the country-side was visited by the drunken wanderings of Pierrots pale in the light of the moon, hideous Borneo apes toting jugs of the local white lightning, lush and cherry-lipped actresses imported from New York, in silk capes, red corsets, long hose; wild Indians, princes of the Renaissance, characters from Dickens, paisley bulls, bears with nosegays; allegorical, garlanded girls named Free Enterprise, Progress, Enlightenment; a giant Maine lobster that never got to extend its claw to the candidate. It snowed, and the last morning of the party a pretty ballet girl dressed as Columbine was found in a quarry nearly dead; the toes of one foot were frostbitten so badly they had to be amputated. She never danced again, and in November Blaine lost the election and was also forgotten. After Baffy died the estate was bought by a retired train robber from Kansas and in 1932 was sold dirt cheap to a chain of hotels which couldn't afford to convert the place and eventually decided that King Yrjö's bucketful of jewels was better than paying the taxes on a white elephant. And now the King too was gone, and the house was empty again, except for the Junta, and one possible cavalry officer.

Hidden among reeds was a flat-bottomed boat they'd found, patched up, and christened the *S. S. Leak*. They piled aboard, and Tim and Étienne rowed. Pierre sat with his paws up on the front end, like a figurehead. Downstream a frog jumped, and falling rain stippled the dark surface of the water. They splashed along under phony-Venetian bridges, some without floorboards so that you could look up and see the gray sky through them; past little landings whose untarred pilings had rotted and collected green slime; an open summerhouse with screening rusted through, which swayed even in soft winds; corroded statues of straight-nosed, fig-leaved youths and maidens, holding horns of plenty, crossbows, impossible Panpipes and stringed instruments, pomegranates, curling scrolls, and one another. Soon, over the tops of leafless willows, the Big House appeared, growing taller the closer they came – more turrets, crenellations, flying buttresses coming into sight at each stroke of the oars. The outside was in fairly lousy shape: a lot of shingling was off, paint had peeled, roof slates lay broken in piles where they'd slid and fallen. Windows had been mostly busted after years of forays by nervous kids double-dared to go in against the cavalry officer and his shotgun. And everywhere the smell of old – eighty-year-old – wood.

They tied the boat to an iron rung sunk in a kind of promenade, went ashore, and trooped around to a side entrance of the Big House. No matter how often they came to the hideout there was a feeling of ceremony, more than any of trespass, about going into the house: It took an effort to step from outside to inside. The inside was full of a pressure, an odor, that resisted intrusions, that kept them conscious of itself until they left again. None of them would go so far as to call it by any name, but they all knew it was there. Part of the ceremony was to look at one another and grin, embarrassed, before pushing on into the twilight that waited for them.

They skirted the edges of the room they'd entered, because hung right in the middle of the ceiling was a cobwebbed, flint-glass chandelier with dust piled in thick stalagmites on its upper facets, and they knew what would happen if you walked under it. The house was full of such mute injunctions: blind places you could be jumped out at from; stretches of warped floor that might suddenly open downward into dungeons or simple dark-nesses with nothing nearby to grab onto; doors that would not stay open behind you but were balanced to close quietly, unless you watched them. These places it was better to stay away from. The route to the hideout was thus like the way into reefed and perilous harbor. If there had been more than four going in, there would have been no danger at all; it would have been just a mob of kids running through an old house. If there had been fewer, it would have been impossible to get beyond the first room.

Creaking, or echoing, or left as dark-ribbed sneaker-prints in a fine layer of damp, the footsteps of the Junta carried them on into King Yrjö's house, past pier glasses that gave them back their images dark and faded, as if some part were being kept as the price of admission; through doorways where old velvet hung whose pile was worn away into maplike patterns, seas and land masses taught in no geography their schools knew; through the scullery, where they'd found a decades-old case of Moxie, of which there were still nine bottles left, Kim Dufay having busted one over the prow of the *S.S. Leak* at its christening, the other two drunk solemnly to celebrate last year's more or less successful Spartacus maneuvers and recently Carl Barrington's membership in the gang; then downstairs, between rows of empty wine racks, into empty utility rooms with empty workbenches and dead electric outlets dangling from overhead in the dark like armless spiders; at last to the house's most secret core, the room behind the ancient coal furnace that they'd found and fixed up and Étienne had spent a week booby-trapping. This is where they met and drew up the time-tables; this is where they kept the sodium under kerosene in a five-gallon can; and the maps with the objectives marked on them, in an old roll-top desk they'd found empty; and the list of public enemies, which no one but Grover had access to.

So the afternoon got darker, the rain came and went in gusts, sometimes thickening to a downpour, then easing off to a drizzle, and deep in the house, in the dry, cold room, the Junta plotted. Their plot had been going on now for three years, and it reminded Tim sometimes of dreams you got when you were sick and feverish, where there was something you had been told to do – find somebody important in an endless strange city full of faces and clues; struggle down the long, inexhaustible network of some arithmetic problem where each step led to a dozen new ones. Nothing ever seemed to change; no "objectives" were taken that didn't create a need to start thinking about new ones, so that soon the old ones were forgotten and let slip by default back into the hands of grownups or into a public no man's land again, and you would be back where you'd started. So what if Étienne (to take a major example) had managed to stop the paper mill last year for almost a week by messing up the water it used? Other things kept on, as if there were something basically wrong and self-defeating with the plot itself. Hogan Slothrop was supposed to have planted a smoke bomb in a PTA meeting the same evening, smoke them out and make off with all their minutes and financial statements, but he'd got a sudden call to go sit with another A.A. member, a stranger in town who had called the local chapter because he was in trouble and afraid.

"What's he afraid of?" Tim had wanted to know.

It had been a year before, in the early fall, a little past the opening of school. Hogan had come over to Tim's house right after supper, and the sky was still light, though the sun was down, and they had been out in Tim's back yard shooting baskets. Or Tim was: Hogan had had this conflict of commitments on his mind.

"Afraid he'll start drinking again," Hogan said, answering Tim's question. "I'm taking this along" – holding up a carton of milk. "If he wants to drink, he can drink this instead."

"Gah," said Tim, who didn't think much of milk.

"Listen," said Hogan, "you never outgrow your need for milk. Let me tell you about milk. How great it is."

"Tell me about beer," Tim said. Being lately fascinated with the idea of getting drunk.

Hogan took offense. "Don't make fun," he said. "I'm lucky I went through that when I did, that's what my father says. Look at this guy I got to go sit with. He's thirty-seven years old. Look at what a head start I got on him."

"You're supposed to plant that smoke bomb tonight," Tim said.

"Come on, Tim, you can do it for me, can't you?"

"Me and Grovie were going to go throw sodium," Tim said. "Remember? It's all got to come off at the same time."

"Well, then, tell Grovie I can't make it," Hogan said. "I'm sorry, Tim, I just can't." At about which point – wouldn't you know? – Grover showed up. They explained to him as diplomatically as they could – which, as usual, wasn't good enough, because Grover flew into a full-scale snit, called them both an assortment of names and stalked off into the darkness which had crept down off the mountains so slow and shifty they hadn't noticed.

"Looks like no sodium-throwing," ventured Hogan, after a while, "huh, Tim?"

"Yeah," said Tim. That's how it always was. Things never went off the way they should've; nothing progressed. Étienne had played frogman that day for nothing, nothing but laughs. The paper mill would start up again, people would go back to work, the insecurity and discontent Grover needed and had counted on for dark reasons he never confided would vanish, and everything would be the way it was.

"Uh come on, Tim," Hogan suggested in his Yogi Bear voice, which he used for cheering people up, "uh why don't you ride down to the hotel, uh and help me sit with this guy?"

"That where he is?" Tim said. Hoge said yeah, the guy was just passing through, and for some reason nobody else wanted to go. Nancy, the secretary at the central A.A. office, had telephoned Hogan as a last resort. When he said OK, she said, "He'll go," to somebody in the office with her, and Hogan heard what sounded like a couple of people laughing.

Tim got his bike, yelled into the house that he'd be back, and they pedaled downhill through the gathering evening and then coasted into the town. It was good fall weather, a borderline time when some trees have jumped the gun and started to change color, and the insects get louder as the days pass, and some mornings, when the wind is out of the Northwest, you can look over, on the way to school, at the higher mountains and make out a few lonely hawks beginning to drift on South, following the crests of the ridges. In spite of all that day's pointlessness, Tim could still enjoy the feeling of coasting down toward the yellow clusters of lights, leaving behind two pages of arithmetic homework and a chapter of science he was supposed to read, not to mention a lousy movie, some romantic comedy dating from the 1940's which was on the only channel you could get up here. As Tim and Hogan zoomed by houses with doors and windows still open for the dark's first coolness they could glimpse the bluish fluorescence of screens, all tuned to the same movie, and pick up snatches of dialogue: ". . . Private, have you gone completely out of your . . ."; ". . . I mean, there *was* a girl back home . . ."; ". . . (splash, comical yell) Oh, sorry, sir, thought you were a Jap infiltrator . . ."; "*How* can I be a Jap infiltrator when we're five thousand . . ."; "I'll wait, Bill, I'll wait for you as long as . . ." and on down, past the firehouse, where a few big kids were sitting around on the old La France engine, telling jokes and smoking, and by the candy store, which neither Tim nor Hogan felt like stopping in tonight, and all of a sudden there were parking meters and several blocks of diagonal parking, which meant you had to put on your brakes and keep an eye out for the traffic., By the time they got to the hotel the night had completely come, had set down on Mingeborough like a lid on a pot, and the stores had begun to close up.

They parked their bikes and went into the lobby. The night clerk, who'd just come on, gave them the fishy eye. "Alcoholics Anonymous?" he said. "You're kidding."

"I swear," said Hogan, showing him the carton of milk. "Call him up. Mr. McAfee, room 217." The clerk, who had the empty night facing him, rang the room and talked to Mr. McAfee. He had a funny look when he hung up.

"Well, it sounds like it's a nigger up there," he informed them.

"Can we go up?" Hogan asked.

The clerk shrugged. "He says he's expecting you. If you have any – you know – trouble, just knock his phone off the hook. See, it'll buzz down here."

"Sure," said Hogan. They went through the empty lobby, between facing rows of armchairs, and got in the elevator. Mr. McAfee was on the second floor. Tim and Hogan looked at each other on the way up but didn't say anything. At his door they knocked for a while before he'd answer. He wasn't much taller than they were. He was a Negro with a small mustache, wearing a gray cardigan and smoking.

"I thought he was kidding," said Mr. McAfee. "You guys really from the A.A.?"

"*He* is," Tim said.

Then something seemed to happen to Mr. McAfee's face. "Oh," he said. "Well, that's pretty funny. They almost as funny up here as they are in Mississippi. OK, you done your bit now? You can go."

"I thought you wanted help," Hogan said, looking puzzled.

Mr. McAfee stood aside. "You're right about that. Yeah. You really want to come in?" He looked like he didn't care. They went in, and Hogan put his milk on the little writing desk in the corner. It was the first time either of them had been in any of the hotel's rooms or spoken to anybody colored.

Mr. McAfee was a bass player, but without his instrument. He'd been over in Lenox at some music festival. He had no idea how he'd got over here.

"It happens sometimes," he said. "I get these blank periods. One minute I was in Lenox. Next thing I know, I show up in – what do you call it? – Mingeborough. That ever happen to you?"

"No," said Hoge. "The worst I ever got was sick."

"You off it now. Alcohol."

"Forever," Hogan said. "Now it's strictly milk."

"Well, that makes you a milko, man," said Mr. McAfee, with a wan smile.

"What am I supposed to do," said Hogan, "exactly?"

"Oh, talk," said Mr. McAfee. "Or I'll talk. Till I can get to sleep. Or somebody – Jill – can get here, come get me, you know?"

"Is that your wife?" Tim said.

"That's who went up the hill with Jack," Mr. McAfee said, and he laughed a little. "No, no kidding, that really happened."

"You want to talk about that?" Hogan said.

"No. I guess not."

So, instead, Tim and Hogan told Mr. McAfee about things like school, and the town, and what their parents did for a living; but soon, because they trusted him, they were also telling him the more secret things – Étienne messing up the paper mill, and the hideout, and the sodium stockpile.

"Yeah," cried Mr. McAfee, "that sodium. I remember.

I threw some in a toilet once – flushed the handle first, you know, then dropped in that sodium. Soon as it hit the water down there, *wham!* That was in Beaumount, Texas, where I used to live. School principal comes walking in the room, very straight face, holding a busted piece of a toilet bowl, like this, and he says, 'Which one of you gentlemen – is responsible – for this outrage?"

Hogan and Tim, giggling, told him about the time Étienne had sat up in a tree with a slingshot, shooting little pea-size sodium balls into the swimming pool at one of the estates during a cocktail party, and the way people scattered at the first explosions.

"Very fancy crowd you run with, there," said Mr. McAfee. "Estates and everything."

"Not us," Tim said. "We just sneak in at night, and swim in the pools then. The one up at Lovelace's estate is the nicest. You want to go there? It's warm enough."

"Yeah," said Hoge. "We could go there now. Come on."

"Well, you know," Mr. McAfee said. He looked embarrassed.

"Why not?" Hoge said.

"Well, you guys should be old enough to know why not," Mr. McAfee said, starting to get mad. He looked at their faces and then shook his head and said, even angrier, "I get caught and that's it, baby. I mean that's all."

"Nobody ever gets caught," Hogan said, trying to reassure him.

Mr. McAfee lay down on the bed and looked at the ceiling. "If they're the right color, nobody gets caught," he said quietly, but the kids heard him.

"So you're a better color than we are," Tim said, "for getting away at night. You're bigger and faster. If we can do it you can, Mr. McAfee, no kidding."

Mr. McAfee looked over at them. He lit another cigarette from the butt of the one he was smoking, never taking his eyes off the two kids. It was hard to tell what he was thinking. "Maybe later," he said after he'd squashed out the old cigarette. "Tell you why I'm nervous about that. It's the water in that pool, see. If you any kind of an alky, it can have a funny effect on you. Ever have that happen, Hogan?" Hogan shook his head no. "Well, I did once, while I was in the army."

"Were you in during World War II?" Tim asked. "Fighting the Japanese or anything?"

"No, I missed that," Mr. McAfee said. "I was too young."

"We missed it too," Hogan told him.

"No, I was in during Korea. Only I stayed Stateside all through it. I was in this band – army band, you know – at Fort Ord, California. All around there, up in the hills around Monterey, you have these little bars; anybody can just walk in, if they want to, and start playing. You have a lot of union guys, used to play around L.A. – you know – they get drafted and sent to Ord. Guys been in studio bands, most of them, so you're sitting in with some fine talent, a lot of times. One night we're in this kind of a roadhouse, four of us, and we're playing, and it's sounding pretty good. We're all juiced a little, drinking wine, there's a lot of wine – you know – from over in that valley there, whatever you call it. We just drinking wine and doing some – oh, some blues or something – and this lady comes in. White lady. Kind that sits out by the swimming pool and drinks cocktails at cocktail parties – right? – yeah. You got it. She's a very stout lady, not big fat, just stout, and she says she wants us to come play at a party she's having. So it's like a Tuesday or a Wednesday and we all kind of curious as to how *come* she's having a party such a funny time of the week, well she says it's been going on since the weekend – nonstop, you know – and we come to find out when we get there she's not putting *no*body on, man. There it is – whooping, hollering, you can hear it for a mile. This baritone sax, some Italian kid, Sheldon somebody, he not halfway in the door there's two or three little chicks all over him, telling him – well, never mind about that – but we set up and get going, and the juice keeps coming on like a bucket brigade, people keep handing it up to you. You know what it is? Champagne. Solid champagne. All night long we drink this stuff, and about the time the sun comes up everybody's passed out, and we quit playing. I lay down next to the drums and go to sleep. Next thing I know I hear this girl, and she's laughing. I get up, the sun's in my eyes, it's only about nine or ten in the morning. I ought to feel horrible, man, but I feel great. I go walking out on this kind of little terrace, it's cold and outside there's fog, not all the way down to the ground, just hiding the tops of the trees, pine trees I guess, the trunks are these – you know – very straight. There's this white fog and downhill there's the ocean. Pacific Ocean, and from up the coast you can even hear that artillery practice back at Ord, wrapped up in the fog, *whoomp, whoomp*. That's how quiet it is. I go on out by the swimming pool, still wondering about this chick I heard laughing, all of a sudden here comes old Sheldon, running out around a corner, with this girl chasing him, and he slams into me, and the girl can't stop in time neither, and we all three of us fall in the pool with all our clothes on. And all I had to do was swallow a little bit of that water and you know what? I'm high all over again, just as high as I was during the night, on all that champagne. How about that?"

"It sounds great," Hogan said. "Except for the alcohol part of it, I mean."

"Yeah, it was great," said Mr. McAfee. "It's the only morning I remember that ever was." He didn't say anything for a while. Then the telephone rang. It was for Tim.

"Hey," said Grover on the other end, "can we come over there? Étienne needs a place to hide tonight." Having, it seems, got second thoughts about his attack on the paper mill earlier that day. It was dawning on him that he'd done something serious, and that the cops, if they got hold of him, would find out about other jobs he'd pulled, and be merciless. Grover's house would be the first place they'd think of to look. It would have to be someplace like the hotel if he wanted to stand a chance of escaping the dragnet. Tim asked Mr. McAfee, who said he guessed so, but reluctant.

"Don't worry," Hogan said. "Étienne's just scared. Like you are."

"Don't you ever get scared?" said Mr. McAfee. His voice had gone funny.

"Not about alcohol," said Hogan. "I guess I was never really that bad."

"Oh, you just passing. I see." He lay still on the bed, his face very black against the pillow. Tim realized that Mr. McAfee had been sweating a lot. It was running off the sides of his neck and soaking into the pillowcase. He looked sick.

"Can I get you anything?" Tim asked, a little worried. When the man didn't answer, he repeated it.

"Just a drink," Mr. McAfee stage-whispered, pointing at Hogan. "See if you can talk your buddy there into letting me have something to relax with. No kidding, I really need something now."

"You can't," Hogan said. "That's the whole point. That's what I'm here for."

"You think that's what you're here for? You wrong." He stood up slowly, as if his stomach or something hurt, and picked up the telephone. "Can you send up a bottle, a fifth, of Jim Beam," he said, "and" – making an elaborate count of the people in the room – "three glasses? Oh.

[*174*]

Right. OK, only one glass. Oh, there is one glass already here." He hung up. "Cat don't miss a trick," he said. "They right on the ball in Mingeborough, Mass."

"Listen, what did you call us up for?" Hogan said. He was talking in an obstinate, rhythmic way that meant he was going to bust out crying any minute. "Why did you get in touch with the A.A. at all, if you were just going to get drunk anyway?"

"I needed help," explained Mr. McAfee, "and I thought they would help me. And they really helped, didn't they? Look at what they sent me."

"Hey," said Tim, and Hogan started to cry.

"OK," said Mr. McAfee. "Out, you guys. Go on home."

Hogan quit crying and got stubborn. "I'm staying."

"The hell you are. Go on. You're the big jokers in town, now you ought to know a joke when you see one. Go back to the A.A. and tell them they really put one over on you, man. Show them you can be – you know – just a gracious loser." Then they all stood looking at each other in the tiny room, with its four-color print of a bowl of chrysanthemums on the wall, its framed list of rules next to the door, its empty, dusty water pitcher and glass, its one armchair, its three-quarter beige-covered bed and its disinfectant smell, and it began to look as if none of them would ever go anyplace, just stand and turn into a kind of wax-museum scene; but then Grover and Étienne showed up, and the other kids let them in. Mr. McAfee made fists at his sides and went to the telephone again. "Get these kids out of here for me," he said, "would you? Please."

Étienne looked as if he were in a state of shock, and about twice as fat as usual. "I think the cops saw us," he kept saying. "Grovie, didn't they?" He was carrying all his skin-diving equipment, which he had an idea would be damning evidence if it were found at his house.

[*175*]

"He's nervous," Grover said. "What's wrong here – you having trouble?"

"We're trying to keep him from starting drinking," Hogan said. "He called A.A. for help, and now he says get out."

"I assume you are aware," Grover addressed the man, "of the positive correlation that exists between alcoholism and heart disease, chronic upper respiratory infection, cirrhosis of the liver – "

"There he is," said Mr. McAfee. In the door, which had been ajar, now appeared Beto Cufifo, the bellboy and town rum-dum, who would have been retired and living on Social Security except that he was Mexican and wanted back there for something like smuggling or auto theft – the charge varied depending on who he was telling it to. How he had first found his way into Berkshire County nobody would ever know. People were always mistaking him for the only kinds of probable outlander – French Canadian or Italian – and you felt he enjoyed that easy ambiguity and that's why he stuck around Mingeborough.

"One bottle of booze," Beto announced. "That's six-fifty."

"What is it, six-fifty, imported from someplace?" Mr. McAfee said. He had out his wallet and snuck a quick look inside. Tim could only see one bill, a single.

"Tell them at the desk," Beto said. "I just carry."

"Look, put it on my room bill, right?" Mr. McAfee said, reaching for the bottle.

Beto put the bottle behind his back. "He says you got to pay now." There were so many lines in his face you couldn't make out the expression too well, but Tim thought he was smiling; a nasty smile. Mr. McAfee took out the dollar and held it up to Beto.

"Come on. Just put it on my tab." Tim could see sweat pouring off him, though nobody else in the room even looked warm.

Beto took the dollar and said, "Now that's five-fifty. I'm sorry. You talk to him down at the desk, sir."

"Hey, you guys," Mr. McAfee said, "any you kids got any bread? I mean I need five and a half – you think you could lend that to me?"

"Not for whiskey," said Hogan, "not even if I had it." The rest of them took out their loose change and held it in their hands and looked to see, but it only came to maybe a dollar and a quarter.

"That still leaves four-twenty-five," announced Beto.

"Oh, you a regular adding machine," yelled Mr. McAfee. "Come on, boy, come on, let's see that bottle."

"You don't believe me," said Beto, gesturing at the telephone, "they'll tell you. Ask them."

For a second it looked like Mr. McAfee might call down. But finally he said, "Look, I'll split it with you, OK? Half that fifth. You must be pretty dry, all that work you do."

"I don't drink this stuff," said Beto. "I'm a wine man. Good night, sir." He started to close the door. Mr. McAfee jumped at him and made a grab for the bottle. Beto, taken by surprise, dropped it. It fell on the rug and rolled a foot or two. Mr. McAfee and Beto had hold of each other's arms and were struggling around, both very clumsy. Hogan picked up the bottle and ran out the door with it and Mr. McAfee saw him and said something like "Oh my God" and tried to get untangled from the bellboy. But by the time he could get to the door, Hogan had too good a head start, and Mr. McAfee must have known that. He just stood with his head on the doorjamb. Beto took out a comb and combed what there was of his hair. Then, hitching up his belt and glaring at Mr. McAfee, he walked around him and out into the hall, and backward all the way to the elevator, watching the colored man as if daring him to try it again.

Grover, Tim and Étienne stood around without knowing exactly what to do. Mr. McAfee had started making a noise in his throat, a sound none of them had heard come from a man before, though Norman, a stray, red kind of puppy who hung around with Pierre times when the hound wasn't sleeping, had once got hold of some chicken bones, which had stuck someplace inside him and Norman had lain out in the dark and made a sound something like it until Grover's father put the dog in his car and drove away with him. Mr. McAfee stood with his head resting on the side of the door, making the same sound. "Hey," Grover said finally, and went over and took the man's hand, which was only a little bigger than Grover's own but dark-colored, and pulled, and Tim said, yeah, come on, and little by little they pulled him away from the door, while Étienne turned down the beige spread on the bed, and they got him to lie down, and put the cover back over him. All of a sudden there was a siren outside. "Cops!" Étienne yelled, and took off for the bathroom. The siren went by the hotel, and Tim looked out and saw it was a fire engine heading out north, and by the time it was quiet in the room again they could hear water running in the bathtub, and Mr. McAfee crying. He'd rolled over on his stomach and was holding the pillow with both hands on either side of his head and crying, the way a little kid cries, sucking air in in a croak, then letting it out in a wail, over and over as if he was never going to stop.

Tim closed the door and sat on the desk chair. Grover sat in the armchair next to the bed, and that was how their night's vigil began. First there was the crying: all

[*178*]

they could do for that was sit and listen. Once the telephone rang. It was the clerk wanting to know if they were having any trouble, and Grover said, "No, he's all right. He'll be all right." Tim had to go in once to the bathroom, and there he found Étienne cowering submerged in a full tub, dressed in his frogman suit, looking like a black watermelon with arms and legs. Tim tapped him on the shoulder and Étienne started to thrash around, trying to go deeper. "No cops," Tim yelled as loud as he could. "It's Tim."

Étienne surfaced and took off his snorkel mask. "I'm hiding," he explained. "I tried to make soapsuds on top but there was only this real little bar of soap, and I guess it all wore off."

"Come on in and help us," Tim said. So Étienne came back in, trailing pools of water all over the place, and sat on the floor; and then the three of them just sat, listening to the man cry. He cried for a long time, and then dozed off. Sometimes he would wake up and talk for long stretches, then sleep again. Now and then one of the kids would drop off too. For Tim it was a little like staying over at Grovie's house and hearing all those cops and merchant captains and barge tenders over the radio, all those voices bouncing off the invisible dome in the sky and down to Grover's antenna and into Tim's dreams. It was as if Mr. McAfee too were broadcasting from somewhere quite distant, telling about things Tim would not be sure of in the daylight: a brother who'd left home one morning during the depression and got on a freight and disappeared, later sending them this one postcard from Los Angeles, and Mr. McAfee, just a boy, deciding to follow him there the same way, only that first time he got no further than Houston; a Mexican girl he'd been with for a while, and she used to drink some stuff all the time, a word Tim couldn't make out, and she had a baby boy who'd died from a rattlesnake bite (Tim saw the snake, headed for him, and bounced up out of the dream in terror, yelling), and so one morning she'd just gone away, like his brother vanished into the same deserted morning, before the sun was even up; and nights when he would sit by himself down around the docks and look off into the black Gulf, where the lights ended, just cut off and left you this giant nothing; and gang scuffles, day after day, up and down the neighborhood streets, or fights out on the beach in the summer's harsh sun; and gigs in New York, L.A., bad gigs with tenor-sax bands it was better to forget only how do you?; cops who'd picked him up, tanks he had known, tankmates with names like Big Knife, Paco-from-the-Moon, one Francis X. Fauntleroy (who'd taken his last wrinkled half a Pall Mall as he slept one evil morning after mixing pot and wine with a projectionist buddy down under a drive-in movie screen outside Kansas City, a big curving thing, while a John Wayne picture exploded overhead).

"*Blood Alley*," Tim said, gentle. "Yeah, I saw it. I saw it too."

Mr. McAfee slept a little then, and came awake remembering aloud another girl he'd met on a bus who played tenor and had just left a white musician she'd been with – this was out of Chicago going west. The two of them sat in the back seat over the motor, singing scat choruses of different things back and forth at each other, and later on in the night she slept on his shoulder and her hair was shiny and sweet, and around Cheyenne she got off and said she guessed she'd go down to Denver, so he never saw her again after that last glimpse of her little figure wandering around the old brick railroad depot across the street from the bus station, among all these ancient cowboy-movie-looking baggage carts, carrying her sax case and waving once at him when the bus pulled out. And he remembered then how he'd left Jill once the same way, only then it had been Lake Charles, Louisiana, back then when Camp Polk was still going strong, and the streets were full of drunken soldiers singing:

Mine eyes have seen the misery of the coming of the draft,
And the day I got the letter was the day I got the shaft.
They said, "My son, we need you,
   'cause the army's understaffed."
And I'm in the F.T.A.

."The what?" said Grover.

"Future Teachers of America," said Mr. McAfee, "very clean-cut organization." And Jill was going on north, to St. Louis or someplace, and he was going back home, back to Beaumont, because his mother was sick. He and Jill had been living in Algiers, across the river from New Orleans, and that time it had been going on two months, not as long as their time in New York, not as short or disastrous as the time in L.A., and this time it had come only to a nostalgic, joint admission that there must be this good-bye at the junction point full of drunks out in the middle of a swamp in the middle of the night. "Hey, Jill," he said. "Hey, baby."

"Who do you want?" Grover said.

"His wife," said Tim.

"Jill?" the man on the bed said. His eyes were closed and he looked as if he were struggling to open them. "Is Jill here?"

"You said she was coming to get you," Tim said.

"No, no, she not coming, man, who told you that?" His eyes flew open suddenly, startling-white. "You got to call her. Hey? Hogan? Call her for me?"

"Tim," Tim said. "What's her number?"

"In my wallet." He took out the wallet, an old brown cowhide one that was bulging apart with papers and stuff. "Here." He looked through it, his fingers scattering things, pulling out old business cards from employment agencies and car dealers and restaurants all across the country, and a calendar from two years ago with dates for University of Texas football games printed on one side, and a four-for-a-quarter photograph of him in his army uniform and smiling, holding a girl in a white coat who was looking down and smiling a little too, and a spare shoelace, and somebody's lock of hair folded into an envelope with part of some hospital's name up in the corner, an old army driver's license that wasn't any good anymore, and a couple of pine needles, a piece of saxophone reed, all kinds of scraps of paper, different colors and shapes. One blue one said "Jill," and had an address in New York, and a telephone number.

"Here." He gave it to Tim. "Call her collect, You know how to make one of them?" Tim nodded. "You got to ask for an outside line. Person-to-person to Miss Jill" – snapping his fingers to call the name back – "ah, Jill Pattison. Yeah."

"It's late," Tim said. "Will she still be up?" Mr. McAfee didn't say anything. Tim got the line, and the long-distance operator, and placed the call. "You don't want me to give them *my* name."

"No, no, tell them Carl McAfee." Then the line seemed to go dead. When it came back on she was ringing. It rang a long time and then a man answered.

"No," he said, "no, she went out the Coast a week ago."

"Do you have another number where she can be reached?" said the operator.

"There's an address someplace." He went away. Silence

fell on the line and it was right around then that Tim's foot felt the edge of a certain abyss which he had been walking close to – for who knew how long? – without knowing. He looked over it, got afraid, and shied away, but not before learning something unpleasant about the night: that it was night here, and in New York, and probably on whatever coast the man was talking about, one single night over the entire land, making people, already so tiny in it, invisible too in the dark; and how hard it would be, how hopeless, to really find a person you needed suddenly, unless you lived all your life in a house like he did, with a mother and father. He turned around to look at the man on the bed and there came to him a hint then of how lost Mr. McAfee really was. What would he do if they couldn't find this girl? And then the man came back and read an address, which Tim copied, and the operator wanted to know if she should try Los Angeles information.

"Yeah," said Mr. McAfee.

"But she can't come get you if she's in Los Angeles."

"But I got to talk to her."

So Tim listened while more clicks and whirs went out like heard fingers, groping across the whole country in the dark, trying to touch one person out of all the millions that lived in it. Finally a girl answered and said she was Jill Pattison. The operator told her she had a collect call from a Carl McAfee.

"Who?" she said.

Somebody knocked on the door, and Grover went and got it. The operator repeated Mr. McAfee's name, and the girl said "Who?" again. There were two policemen at the door. Étienne, who'd been sitting behind the bed, gave a yelp and scuttled away into the bathroom and jumped back in the tub with a great splash.

"Leon, down at the desk, thought we ought to look in," one of the cops said. "Did this man bring you kids up here?"

"The clerk knows he didn't," Grover said.

"What should I – " Tim said, waving the phone.

"Hang up," said Mr. McAfee. "Forget it." He tightened his hands into fists and lay looking at the cops.

"Fella," said the other cop, "bellboy says you didn't have the price of a bottle of whiskey a while ago."

"That's right," said Mr. McAfee.

"Room here's seven dollars a night. How were you going to pay for that?"

"I wasn't," said Mr. McAfee. "I'm a vagrant."

"Come on," said the first cop.

"Hey," Tim said, "you can't. He's sick. Call the A.A. – they know about him."

"Cool off, son," said the other cop. "He's going to get a nice free room tonight."

"Call Doctor Slothrop," Tim said. The cops had taken Mr. McAfee off the bed and were moving him toward the door.

"My things?" he said.

"Somebody'll take care of them. Come on. You kids too. It's time you were getting home."

Tim and Grover followed them down the hall, into the elevator, out through the lobby past the clerk and into the empty street, where the cops put Mr. McAfee into a patrol car. Tim wondered if either of their voices had ever come over the radio rig at Grover's, had ever figured in any of his dreams. "Be careful," he yelled at them. "He's real sick. You got to take care of him."

"Oh, we'll take care of him," said the cop who wasn't driving. "He knows it too, don't he? Look at him." Tim looked. All he could see were the whites of eyes, and cheekbones highlighted in sweat. Then the car took off, leaving the odor of rubber and a long screech hanging at the curb. That was the last they saw of him. They went down to the station house next day, but the cops said he'd been taken to Pittsfield, and there was no way at all of knowing whether they were telling the truth.

A few days later the paper mill started up again, and then there was that year's Operation Spartacus to worry about, and then the idea Nunzi Passarella came up with of getting car batteries from Étienne's father's junkyard, and a couple of old surplus spotlights and some sickly green cellophane, and rigging the lights up by the railroad cut just outside Mingeborough where the train had to slow down for a curve, getting at least fifty kids to put on rubber monster masks of various kinds, and capes and homemade bat outfits and such, then sit around on the slopes of the cut until the train came, switching on the sickly green spotlights just as it appeared around the curve, and see what happened. Only half the expected number of kids showed up but it was still a success, the train coming to a horrible grinding halt, ladies screaming, conductors yelling, Étienne cutting the lights and the kids fleeing away up the sides of the cut and into the fields. Grover, who'd been sporting a zombie mask of his own design, had afterward said something curious: "I feel different now and better for having been green, even sickly green, even for a minute." Though they never talked about it, Tim felt the same way.

In the spring he and Étienne hopped a freight train for the first time in their lives, and rode to Pittsfield to see a merchant name of Artie Cognomen, a stout, poker-faced, onetime Bostonian who looked like a selectman and smoked a pipe with a bowl carved in the shape of Winston Churchill's head, complete with cigar. Artie sold practical jokes. "Have a very nice dribble glass in with the spring consignment," he informed them. "Also a wide selection in whoopee cushions, exploding cigars –" "No," said Étienne. "What kind of disguises you got?" Artie showed them all he had – wigs, fake noses, glasses with bug eyes on them – but what they finally settled for was a couple of mustaches you could clip to your nose and two little tins of blackface makeup. "You guys must be reactionaries or something," Mr. Cognomen told them. "This stuff has been sitting around for years. It may even have turned white. You trying to resurrect vaudeville or something?" "We're trying to resurrect a friend," Étienne answered right back without thinking, and then he and Tim looked at each other in surprise, as if some fourth person in the room had said it.

Then this summer the Barringtons had moved into Northumberland Estates, and the kids, as usual, had advance word on it. Their parents suddenly seemed to spend more time talking about the coming of the Barringtons than anything else. They began to use words like "blockbusting" and "integration."

"What's integration mean?" Tim asked Grover.

"The opposite of differentiation," Grover said, drawing an x-axis, y-axis and curve on his greenboard. "Call this function of x. Consider values of the curve at tiny little increments of x" – drawing straight vertical lines from the curve down to the x-axis, like the bars of a jail cell – "you can have as many of these as you want, see, as close together as you want."

"Till it's all solid," Tim said.

"No, it never gets solid. If this was a jail cell, and those lives were bars, and whoever was behind it could make himself any size he wanted to be, he could always make himself skinny enough to get free. No matter how close together the bars were."

"This is integration," said Tim.

"The only kind I ever heard of," said Grover. Late that night they tuned in on Grover's parents' bedroom, to see if they could find out any thing new about the Negro family that was coming.

"They're worried up there," Mr. Snodd said. "They don't know whether to start selling now or try and stick it out. All it takes is one to panic."

"Well," said Grover's mother, "thank God they don't have any children, or there'd be a panic in the PTA, too."

Intrigued, they sent Hogan in to the next PTA meeting to see what was up. Hogan reported back the same thing: "They say there's no kids this time, but they ought to be looking ahead and making plans in case it ever does happen."

It was hard to see what their parents were all so scared of. As it turned out, not only scared but also misinformed. The day after the Barringtons finally did move in, Tim, Grover and Étienne went up to their house after school just to look around. They found the house no different from any others in the development; but then, leaning against a steel street light, watching them, they saw the kid. He was kind of rangy and dark, and he was wearing a sweater, even though it was warm out. The others introduced themselves and said they were going up to the overpass to drop water balloons on cars, and would he like to come along?

"What's your name?" Étienne said.

"Well," said the kid, snapping his fingers for it, "it's Carl. Yeah, *Carl* Barrington." Turned out he had a perfect eye for getting water balloons to splat right on a guy's windshield. They went over to the junkyard later and fooled around with ball bearings and busted automatic-transmission units, and then walked Carl home. The next day he was in school, and every day after that. He sat quietly in a seat in the corner that had been empty, and the teacher never called on him, though he was as smart as Grover on some things. A week or so later Grover learned the other meaning for integration, from watching Huntley and Brinkley, the only television show he ever looked at.

"It means white kids and colored kids in the same school," Grover said.

"Then we're integrated," Tim said. "Hey."

"Yeah. They don't know it, but we're integrated."

Then Tim's and Grover's folks, and even, according to Hogan, the progressive Doctor Slothrop, started in with the telephone calls, and the name-calling, and the dirty words they got so angry with kids for using. The only parent who was keeping out of it seemed to be Étienne's father. "He says why don't people stop worrying about Negroes and start worrying about automation," Étienne reported. "What's automation, Grovie?"

"I start studying it next week," said Grover. "I'll tell you then." But he didn't, because by that time they were all involved again with the arrangements for this year's Spartacus maneuvers. They began to spend more and more time up at the hideout at King Yrjö's, plotting. They knew by now, their third year at it, that the reality would turn out to be considerably less than the plot, that something inert and invisible, something they could not be cruel to or betray (though who would have gone so far as to call it love?) would always be between them and any clear or irreversible step, as much as the powdery fiction of the school's outline on Fazzo's Field had stopped the little kids last year. Because everybody on the school board, and the railroad, and the PTA and paper mill had to be somebody's mother or father, whether really or as a member of a category; and there was a point at which the reflex to their covering warmth, protection, effectiveness against bad dreams, bruised heads and simple loneliness took over and made worthwhile anger with them impossible.

Still, the four of them sat now in the secret room, which had grown cold with the approach of night, while Pierre, the basset hound, nosed restlessly in the corners. They agreed that Carl would run a time-motion study on letting air out of tires in the shopping center's parking lot, and Étienne would make more of an effort to obtain parts for the gigantic sodium catapult Grover had designed; and that Tim could begin each run-through of Operation Spartacus with a few more limbering-up exercises, taking the Royal Canadian Air Force plan as a point of departure. Grover allotted them the personnel they felt they would need, and then at last they adjourned. In single file they reran the house's gauntlet of shadows, resonances and dread possibilities, came out into the rain which had not stopped, and re-embarked on the *S. S. Leak.*

They rowed her as far as the culvert under the state highway, then walked through that, and skirted around a piece of the swamp to Fazzo's Field, to check out the maneuver site. Then they went over to the stretch of track beyond the point designated Foxtrot, and crouched among barren shadbushes whose berries they had eaten earlier in the year, and lobbed rocks down on the tracks to see how the angle of fire was. They couldn't tell too much because there was hardly any light left to the sky. So they walked the tracks back almost to the Mingeborough station, then cut over into town, where they came trailing into the candy store, beginning to feel a little tired, sat in a row at the empty counter and ordered four lemon-limes with water. "Four?" said the lady behind the fountain. "Four," said Grover, and as usual she gave them a funny look. For a while they hung around the revolving wire racks, looking through comics; then they walked Carl home, through the quickening rain.

Even before they reached the Barringtons' block they felt something was wrong. Two cars and a pickup truck trailing garbage came tearing by from that direction, windshield wipers batting furiously, tires sending up wings of water that splashed the kids even though they jumped up on one of the lawns. Tim looked over at Carl, but Carl didn't say anything.

When they got to Carl's house they found the front lawn littered with garbage. For a while they only stood; then, as if compelled to do so, began kicking through it, looking for clues. The garbage was shin-deep all over the lawn, neatly spread right up to the property line. They must have brought it all in the pickup. Tim found the familiar A&P shopping bags his mother always brought home, and the skins of some big yellow oranges an aunt had sent them as a gift from Florida, and the pint box of pineapple sherbet Tim himself had bought two nights ago, and all the intimacy of the throwaway part, the shadow-half of his family's life for all the week preceding, the crumpled envelopes addressed to his father and mother, the stubs of the black De Nobili cigars his father liked to smoke after supper, the folded beer cans, always with the point coming in between the two e's of the word "beer," exactly the way his father did and had taught him how to do — ten square yards of irrefutable evidence. Grover was going around unfolding papers and turning over things and finding out that his garbage was there too. "And Slothrops' and Mostlys'," Étienne reported, "and I guess a lot of people from around the development here, too."

They'd been picking up garbage for about five minutes, throwing it in cans they found by the carport, when the front door opened and Mrs. Barrington started yelling at them.

"But we're cleaning it up," Tim said. "We're on your side."

"We don't need your help," the woman said. "We don't need any of you on our side. I thank our heavenly Father every day of my life that we don't have any children to be corrupted by the likes of you trash. Now get out, go on now." She started to cry.

Tim shrugged and threw away an orange peel he was holding. He considered getting a beer can to confront his father with, but then figured all that would get him was spanked, and hard, so he forgot about it. The three of them walked away, slowly, looking back now and then at the woman, who was still standing in her doorway. They'd gone two blocks before they realized that Carl was still with them.

"She didn't mean it," he said. "She just – you know – mad."

"Yeah," said Tim and Grover.

"I don't know" – the boy, now almost faded into the rain, gestured back at the house – "if I should go in now, or what. What should I do?"

Grover, Tim and Etienne looked at one another. Grover, as spokesman, said, "Why don't you lay low for a while?"

"Yeah," Carl said. They walked down to the shopping center and across the slick black parking lot that reflected greenish mercury-vapor lights, and a red supermarket sign, and a blue gas-station sign, and many yellow lights. They walked among these colors on the wide black pavement that seemed to stretch to the mountains.

"I guess I'll – you know – go up to the hideout, then," Carl said, "up to King Yrjö's place."

"At night?" Étienne said. "What about the calvary officer?"

"Cavalry," said Grover.

"He won't bother me," said Carl. "You know."

"We know," said Tim. Sure they did: Everything Carl said, they knew. It had to be that way: He was what grownups, if *they'd* known, would have called an "imaginary playmate." His words were the kids' own words; his gestures too, the faces he made, the times he had to cry, the way he shot baskets; all given by them an amplification or grace they expected to grow into presently. Carl had been put together out of phrases, images, possibilities that grownups had somehow turned away from, repudiated, left out at the edges of towns, as if they were auto parts in Étienne's father's junkyard – things they could or did not want to live with but which the kids, on the other hand, could spend endless hours with, piecing together, rearranging, feeding, programming, refining. He was entirely theirs, their friend and robot, to cherish, buy undrunk sodas for, or send into danger, or even, as now, at last, to banish from their sight.

"If I like it," Carl said, "I might stay there awhile too." The others nodded, and then Carl broke loose and took off at a jogging run across the lot, waving his hand without looking back. When he'd vanished in the rain, the three kids put their hands in their pockets and started back for Grover's house.

"Grovie," said Étienne, "are we still integrated? If he doesn't come back? Hops a freight somewhere or something?"

"Ask your father," said Grover. "I don't know anything." Étienne picked up a handful of wet leaves and stuffed them down Grover's back. Grover kicked water at him but missed and splashed Tim. Tim jumped up and shook a branch, showering Grover and Étienne. Étienne tried to push Tim over Grover, who'd got down on all fours, but Tim caught on and pushed Grover's face in the mud. That was how they left the lights of the shopping center and took leave of Carl Barrington, abandoning him to the old estate's other attenuated ghosts and its precarious shelter; and rollicked away into that night's rain, each finally to his own house, hot shower, dry towel, before-bed television, good night kiss, and dreams that could never again be entirely safe.

"The Small Rain" was first published in
the *Cornell Writer* of March 1959.

"Low-lands" was first published in
New World Writing 16 in March 1960.

"Entropy" was first published in
the *Kenyon Review* in Spring 1960.

"Under the Rose" was first published in
The Noble Savage 3 in May 1961.

"The Secret Integration" was first published in
The Saturday Evening Post in December 1964.